The Gods Return

Flaming Janet

Shadow of Palaces

Marjorie of Scotland

Here Lies Margot

Maddalena

Forget Not Ariadne

Julia

The Devil of Aske

The Malvie Inheritance

The Incumbent

Whitton's Folly

Norah Stroyan

The Green Salamander

Tsar's Woman

Homage to a Rose

Stranger's Forest

Daneclere

Daughter of Midnight

Fire Opal

Knock at a Star

A Place of Ravens

This Rough Beginning

The House of Cray

The Fairest One of All

Duchess Cain

Bride of Ae

The Copper-Haired Marshal

Still Blooms the Rose

The Governess

Children of Lucifer

Sable for the Count

My Lady Glamis

Venables

The Sisters

Digby

Fenfallow

The Sutburys

Jeannie Urquhart

The Woman in the Cloak

Artemia

Trevithick

The Loves of Ginevra

Vollands

A Dark Star Passing

The Brocken

The Sword and the Flame

Mercer

The Silver Runaways

Angell & Sons

Aunt Lucy

O Madcap Duchess

The Parson's Children

The Man from the North

Journey Beyond Innocence

The Charmed Descent

The Inadvisable Marriages

Curtmantle

Murder in Store

The Supplanter

Countess Isabel

The Lion's Daughter

Bailie's Wake

The Gods Return

PAMELA HILL

ROBERT HALE · LONDON

© Pamela Hill 2000
First published in Great Britain 2000

ISBN 0 7090 6552 3

Robert Hale Limited
Clerkenwell House
Clerkenwell Green
London EC1R 0HT

The right of Pamela Hill to be identified as
author of this work has been asserted by her
in accordance with the Copyright, Designs and
Patents Act 1988.

2 4 6 8 10 9 7 5 3 1

Typeset by
Derek Doyle & Associates, Liverpool.
Printed in Great Britain by
St Edmundsbury Press, Bury St Edmunds, Suffolk.
Bound by WBC Book Manufacturers Limited, Bridgend

The Gods Return

I
Founding Fathers

1

AARON MASTERSON, potter, was eighty-seven years old and had recently begun to allow himself to admit the fact. His shrewd, solid old face resembled crumpled paper that has been left to turn yellow, though his hands were as strong and cunning as ever. These days he was largely unseen about the pottery itself, which had gone from strength to strength in the course of three reigns; but remained the puppet-master pulling strings from behind a curtain. The curtain was Victorian and respectable, chosen by Aaron's second wife. It boasted particularly hideous bobble trimming.

Old Aaron sat in the leather armchair he had long worn shiny with use, aware as always of each beat of the nearby pottery's pulse, the throwing, the moulding, the firings. Orders had come gradually from customers in England and, when the war with Napoleon was ended, from abroad despite the prohibitions and tariffs of Europe's new masters. The firm of Masterson and Bevan was as well known as Wedgwood by now, and had made more money by ignoring international law and running a private fleet of ships.

While he turned the accounts over in his mind, the old man stared, as always lately, at a glazed figurine of a young woman. It was about twenty-two inches high, and a subtle honey colour. It was a model of his long-dead love, Sophy Southern. Nathan, his erstwhile partner now retired, had made it. Sophy had been Nathan's sister, though much younger.

Nathan Bevan. Aaron's face grew bitter, his eyes deep with resentment. He had always known he had no control over the Fates. They had forced him, in the form of insistence from puritanical Nathan, to return Sophy to her husband, who had thereafter beaten her to death.

He brooded over the memory, the abomination of it. Walter Southern had been hanged, as was right and proper. He, Masterson, had thrown his mind again into his work, which was concerned with clay. Over the years he had taken other women, but loved none. The sons they had borne him were by now managers in the firm or else they marketed, at home and for export, the various aspects the pottery firm had achieved over seventy-odd years.

It would have fared less well, become less prosperous and unique, without the presence of Nathan Bevan. This had never been pleasant; there was something about the man that made women shrink. No doubt it was the effect of the odd sect to which Bevan had belonged; a few of them were scattered about, some employed in the pottery, but they had limitations as to what they would and wouldn't make; if it was ungodly, they wouldn't touch it. Nathan himself had refused to continue in partnership unless Aaron's sinful liaison, as he called it, with another man's wife came to an end.

It had been a question of heart versus head. Nathan's knowledge of glazes would never be surpassed; he was turning out marvellous and unrivalled blues and greens, and orders were piling up. Aaron had told himself that Sophy was, after all, one more woman, but there was no second Nathan; and so Nathan had led Sophy away. What had happened after that was blackness, not to be remembered, and a few years after, Nathan had begun to go blind. He was of no further use, and Aaron told him to go back to his sect in the north, sending him money from shares from time to time. Nathan had left his glaze receipts behind, all except the one for the figurine and the bowl; he would not part with either, and Aaron had contrived a similar one, though less subtle, for the purposes of commerce, and continued alone. Nathan's deft, laconic presence had been missed less than his knowledge, despite the assurance with which he designed and threw bowls, vases, platters, jugs with spouts and handles not emulated since the days of ancient Crete. His work had been unique, but they could of course copy it by now in plaster moulds. Otherwise, it could be said Sophy's life had been bartered to retain her brother's talent for the firm.

If he, Masterson, had this earthly life to live over again, would he act differently? He knew that he would not. Money and success meant more to him than anything in the world. He was a hard man. He had made two marriages, both to well-dowered women. The first had produced Olave, whose mother had died three years after, of a blockage. The second – Margaret was still alive, forty years his junior and with false teeth, while he still had his own – the second had produced only Clara. Both daughters were damned ugly women, although Olave at least had brains. He had contrived, by means of handsome dowries, to marry them well enough. Olave had married a bishop, Clara the heir of an earl. Both had sons.

It was the vengeance of the Fates that he, Masterson, should have no legitimate son of his own. Maybe if he had seen the

11

daughters married younger there might have been a choice of grandson he approved; as it was, one was a fool and the other a wastrel. He had however been too provident, anxious lest the business fall into the hands of fortune-hunters. He grimaced. Sophy, had matters turned out other than they had, would have borne him fair sons and daughters. She had been beautiful, and he had, at that time, possessed a certain rugged handsomeness. Slender ivory limbs, she'd had, fit for caressing rather than beating; hair of spun gold, spread out over the pillow on which they lay. Her eyes – he could see them now – had had an oblique slant to them, the colour of ripe filberts between her long dark-gold lashes; she hadn't had white lashes and invisible brows, like most fair women. During their lovemaking the lashes would lie idle on her smooth cheeks. He felt love stir now, and desire, even though he was old, so very old, these days, this century. The age he had reached continued to gratify him; nothing surprised him now.

They had been promised to one another, he and Sophy, in the early days before he had made his name and fortune. That had come with the discovery, by Nathan, of a leopard-skin glaze which rivalled the old inconvenient method with salt; it had become fashionable and had remained so till perhaps ten years ago, when tastes had changed. He had been ready by then with some other novelty. Whatever passion remained in him was for his craft, and the making of money.

If he had had money earlier, Sophy's family would have let them marry. They'd been well-found, with a fortune made from the slave trade in the old days. They hadn't considered him a suitable match as things were, and when Southern had offered for her, being of the same religious persuasion – Aaron himself had no religion – they had forced the other marriage. A short time after, there had been a night of storm and rain; and out of it she had come shivering in to him, with a shawl flung over her nightdress, nothing more. He had taken her straight to bed and had seen the bruises on her arms and body. 'You shall not leave me again,' he had promised; and then had let her brother Nathan cause him to break his word. In a way, though, she had never left him, for he remembered her still; and nowadays gazed at the figurine by the hour.

Gravel beyond the clay seam had been found after she'd been returned to Southern, and its possibilities had been extended, with a refinery for the filtered dust, to make the hardest stoneware in England. Nathan had gone off to Germany for a year to study the high firings needed for kaolin, and had brought a consignment, and much knowledge, back with him. If the seam of original clay here ran out – and after all these years it showed no sign of being worked to its end, it was a richer deposit than any in the Potteries – he, Aaron, had other options. By now, he had links with Saxony himself, and could produce porcelain as fine as they made in Meissen. He had invested in profitable land; he had fields growing flax, had invested in Indian cotton in time to avert the ruin that overtook many during the late wars with France. All things had turned to gold under his hand, like King Midas. He'd had asses' ears, that king; and had mistakenly turned his own daughter into gold. Well, that had hardly happened with Clara and Olave; the earl's son spent a good deal on collecting rare editions, and as for the bishop, he gave money away right and left; fortunately a certain amount was tied up for the two women. Olave had climbed socially somewhat further than Clara; trade wasn't admitted into the aristocracy, but the old earl had an odd streak and supported Bonaparte. Well, the Corsican had had his points. No doubt class barriers would

13

tumble sooner or later, as they had among the French, at least on the surface. He hadn't, himself, found time to cross the Channel, and now never would.

He moved in the leather chair, restlessly. He hadn't been present when Nathan took Sophy back to her husband. He had stayed away, knowing he would be unable to resist her pleading, whereas Nathan had his grim righteousness to sustain him. Nathan and he had been closer friends before all that than afterwards. Later, they were merely partners in the business. Nathan had never married.

That death . . . and his own, surely to come soon now. No man could expect to live much longer than he had done, giving himself to his work. He'd only retired of recent years, when standing at the wheel had tired him. He still threw the occasional pot.

Would she be waiting for him in the place where souls were? He had never believed in God. If he was wrong, and there was a life beyond this one, what would she say?

'I trusted you, and you betrayed me. You let me go back because of the money Nathan could make for you. You cared more for that than for me, though you said you loved me. You have made money and more money since then, but what will you do with it? Has it brought you happiness? Have you been happy since we last lay together, except at your wheel, your eternal wheel? You could forget everything then. You were always the same. No woman could ever mean as much to you as a wheel, and clay.'

If there was a heaven, and he wouldn't reach it, there was no lovemaking, no marrying, there. They would float, perhaps, the two of them, forever on the wind, like the pair of lovers in Dante who had sinned. Oh, he'd educated himself. It was pointless to

14

remember and repine. He was a hypocrite in any case; he went, had always gone for the look of the thing, with Margaret to church on Sundays, It was one way of making business contacts; and it gave Margaret an opportunity to show off both the girls, when they were young, with rich velvet dresses and hats, and fur pelisses and muffs, or straw and flowers in summer. It made up for their plain faces. It made clear to everyone that the pottery was doing well.

Margaret his wife came in now, moving listlessly as she always did lately, not that there seemed anything wrong with her. She was a thin, grave woman who had never had looks to lose, and did not dress fashionably herself She wore a plain grey gown of heavy faille with a bertha of Brussels lace, and her iron-grey hair was released from its fierce nightly curling-rags to cascade beneath her cap. She asked for his health.

'I'm as usual,' he grunted. 'What did you expect?'

Margaret didn't add that she expected nothing, and never had after the first, when it had been made clear there was no affection in her marriage. She did her duty and had from the commencement. She hadn't minded his unfaithfulnesses except for that sudden infatuation, years ago now, for a handsome workman named George who used to keep the clay moist in the bins. In the end the bishop, her elder daughter Olave's husband, had quietly paid the young man's fare to Canada, where he was still. Aaron had been persuaded that scandal would be bad for business. Nothing else would have affected him.

She saw that he was gazing, as usual, at the little glazed figurine on the escritoire. It seemed to have some meaning for him. One day, if the housemaids were careless, it might break. Perhaps it should be put under glass.

15

*

As soon as she had gone, the old man rose from his leather chair and stumped over to the windows, looking out past their prosperously fringed and draped curtains. Within sight, though not too near the house itself, were the offices and what was, by this time, almost a village of great outdoor kilns. Some were being raked out at present now the ashes had cooled from last night's firing. It was not yet time to open the doors on the cooling ware, made commercially from casts; results there were predictable. The men at work looked like ants from here. Further off there were fires still lit, for the glost firing. He knew the site of those special kilns, which had been Nathan's pride. In the end, it had cost Nathan his eyesight; the constant bending and working with chemicals and great heat, the enthralling moment when, through the viewing-hole, the glazes could be seen to run and melt and shine. Whatever mystery had transpired in that intense heat would not be revealed for two further days, days of impatience that passed slowly, but to open everything too soon might mean cracks and ruin from the cold outer air. There had been discoveries made in those days, accidents of shade and speckling from some chance element in the burning charcoal; or subtle unexpected colours from a prescribed receipt which had decided, for itself, to change in the kiln, for the colours to fly from one shelf to the next. Those pieces were prized rarities now, which fetched a high price from collectors. Nathan had rightly gone when his sight went, agreeing that he was useless; he'd returned willingly enough to his own strict sect in the north. They hadn't kept in touch, except to send up Nathan's share as partner still. He, Aaron, hoped to make further experiments of his own now there was this new piped gas in cities. It made

16

humanity look corpse-like in the gaslit streets, but might produce brilliant colours under reduction. No doubt he himself – he grinned – would be a corpse before a gasometer could be erected near enough the offices.

All of it must go then; but to whom?

2

CLARA, Viscountess Tenterdowne – she had been Clara Masterson once – stole cautiously about among the library shelves at Lawley, handing the valuable editions with great care. Her husband John, immersed as usual in his reading, sat at his desk, his handsome grey head – the hair had turned that colour quite young, otherwise he looked like Apollo except for reading-spectacles – bent, and ignored her as usual. Clara worshipped him, but knew only too well that her father's money, with its prospect of purchasing as many books as John Tenterdowne chose, was the reason why he had married her. She knew that she had few attractions, and thankfully Tenterdowne did not look at other women, or gamble or back horses; but rare books were his passion. Lately he had permitted her to assist him in indexing what was becoming a notable library. She had grasped at this crumb with pathos; at least she could admire his profile while he was unaware.

Indexing – she had turned out to be efficient at it – and the money apart, she was a failure and knew it. Their only son – Charley's birth had been so difficult there could never be others – was a great lumpish creature, eight years old now, with his tutors upstairs. He was amiable, but not very bright, and had to be educated privately. He would never have endured the rough-and-tumble of school, and they would have mocked him for being too fat.

He had been christened Charles after the earl, her husband's father, with whom they lived and who was almost of an age now with Papa, though not quite. The earl had odd views which caused him to be unpopular in society. He believed Waterloo to have been a disaster for the English nation and that it would have been of benefit had Napoleon won. 'We'd have had proper roads then, and a proper government, and that handsome boy with fair hair and brains as our future king, not a gouty lecher and then a madman, and now their rabbit-mouthed niece and her German husband. What happened instead? The King of Rome died of lung-rot and a broken heart in Austria, where his bitch of a mother should never have taken him. Shouldn't have left Paris, boy clung to the door-handle, didn't want to go, only three at the time, knew already what he wanted. It's a good thing to know what you want early in life.' The earl had glared up at her then from the bath-chair wherein he preferred to sit these days, although he could still walk in for dinner and drive the pony-trap. On Clara's relating his father's notions to her husband, Tenterdowne had remarked bitterly that he knew the old devil's views perfectly well, they had ruined his boyhood and youth as nobody would invite him anywhere. He didn't add that that was why he had married herself, a tradesman's daughter with enough money to allow him to read for the rest of his existence. Clara had listened obediently, her heart breaking. Perhaps, if she carried out this indexing with perfection, he might become a little fond of her.

It didn't look like it. 'Fetch me volume 9 of 123,' remarked the viscount coldly from his desk, without looking up. How young he seemed, much younger than forty-two! He had been twelve years old when Waterloo was fought, and she herself five years older still.

Looking in the glass upstairs Clara often felt despair; she didn't have a single engaging feature. Olave, who wasn't pretty either, at least had a certain amount of social life as the bishop's helpmeet, though their son was a vicious young creature, albeit handsome, with that red hair.

She found 123, volume 9, and in taking it to the desk stumbled unwittingly on the carpet's edge. 'Take care of that, it's worth almost a thousand pounds,' said Tenterdowne testily. He didn't mean the carpet. Clara could have replied that the thousand pounds was hers, or rather had been. The money, in plain fact, was disappearing rapidly as the library grew. There wouldn't be much left for poor Charley unless he made a rich marriage of his own.

Tenterdowne himself was an aesthete, and had from the beginning found his marriage distasteful; he couldn't even stand the sound of Clara's voice, it was like gravel in one of the new tin cans. He blamed the earl for having smuggled out large sums of the family inheritance to aid Napoleon during the Hundred Days. His outspoken beliefs, then and afterwards – he said it was cruelty to keep so brilliant a mind chained to a remote rock, worse than Prometheus, and if they'd had the sense to let his wife and son go to him on Elba he mightn't have left it – had resulted in ostracism; John Tenterdowne, growing up, felt this more keenly than his father, who had developed an interest in pig-breeding. The vulgar marriage had been the only option, to a young woman almost past matrimony; Tenterdowne had consummated the marriage with disdain and had been thankful for the prompt commencement of Charley; at least that was that.

'You need not wait,' he said somewhat cruelly now to Clara, of whose adoration he was aware and which irritated him like everything else about her. He opened the book she had at least delivered safely, and rid of her heavy breathing over his shoulder began to revel in the black-letter text with its hand-coloured plates, some of them engravings by Dürer and Cranach. Tenterdowne wondered at times if his father's Francophile inclinations had driven him himself into the arms of Germany, which country was, nowadays, an ally still.

He stared down at the slim virginal Cranachs. He had never beheld perfect female beauty in the flesh, and the little unripe apples of breasts portrayed aroused no feeling in him other than a scholar's chilly assessment. If such a young woman were before him now, he thought, he would educate her to recite poetry of a kind to cause her breasts to ripen somewhat. The thought made him smile thinly. It was a chimera, no more; the kind of thing that passed his days rather than his nights, when he slept soundly and alone.

Clara had meantime crept carefully upstairs lest the stairs' creaking disturb Tenterdowne at his reading. To please him in every possible way would have been her life's desire, but as it was the best thing that she could do was to avoid displeasing him if possible. She paused on the landing to look in at her son, who by now was practising copperplate, his tongue weaving laboriously back and forth beyond his lips. He looked up, hearing her, smiled in a friendly way, and beamed short-sightedly with amiable blue-grey eyes, his best feature. He would never be good at anything. 'He is working hard, I trust,' said Clara to the tutor, referring to her son, as most did, in the third person although present.

21

The tutor made some suitable reply, and Clara passed on and upwards. She had a little tower room to herself, in which she sat when dismissed from the library and indulged in Berlin crewel work, knowing Tenterdowne liked all things German. She was in fact working laboriously on a pair of slippers for his birthday. Perhaps he would be pleased. She sat down and began to stitch patiently at the ugly reds and cabbage greens, making sure there were no uncomfortable knots at the back. Soon it would be time for luncheon, and Tenterdowne and the earl would both be present and they would all eat in silence because there was nothing left to say. Charley ate with the tutor in the schoolroom, as was customary.

Forty-seven miles due east from Viscount Tenterdowne's expanding library at Lawley, Clara's sister Olave, the bishop's wife, who resembled their father Aaron more closely than her younger sister – Olave would never have given in to a husband's whims – sat dominating the Ladies' Sewing Circle for Foreign Missions. The bishop, having made a brief and benevolent appearance to open the meeting with prayer, had retired to his study in the cathedral close.

The ladies, their skirts spread prosperously to show off varied braid trimmings, were mostly comfortable mothers of families which could safely be left with the servants. There were, in addition, certain dispirited elder daughters it was probably too late to marry. Everyone sewed industriously under the firm eye of Olave Pallant, and nobody present was conversant enough with the seamier side of life to realise that the scene resembled a women's prison with the inmates sewing mail-bags under the narrow supervision of a wardress. In fact, the effort on the whole, though modish, was pointless; the black and brown persons for whom the calico garments were intended looked much better as nature had made them. However, the local poor were sent flannel underwear at Christmas, which was helpful.

Olave's charity was all-embracing and she made the bishop an excellent, if overpowering, wife: neither he nor she were exactly certain how it had happened. Having taken place, the marriage had, like poor Clara's, produced one son. It was accepted that the marital act was for the procreation of children only, and as Olave was older than Clara it was probable that young Ivor was quite enough. Clever and handsome as he was, Ivor had already proved a hideous disappointment to his father, having lately been expelled from school for unmentionable reasons. As the school had been a prestigious one for the sons of clergy, there was little hope of containing the disgrace.

Olave considered the matter while she sewed. It was difficult to know what would become of Ivor now; perhaps Cambridge was out of the question, given his known contempt of all discipline and the further temptations offered there. One recalled how the late Lord Byron – his name was naturally not mentioned openly any more despite the undoubted post-mortem feat of Greek independence – had squandered, within weeks, all his mother had scrimped and saved over the years to try to safeguard his inheritance. Ivor would unquestionably behave in the same way, and be sent down almost as soon as he had been sent up, There was, accordingly, no point in wasting money; the bishop's charities were quite enough, and he had no sense of economy, good soul, at all.

Hearing with half her mind the subdued murmur of genteel conversation and even occasionally taking part, Olave considered the wisdom, or otherwise, of sending Ivor to Lawley to share the tutor his cousin Charley, or rather Charley's grandfather, had selected. However Charley was not only younger, but mentally slow, which nobody could say about Ivor; the latter had a flair for languages and picked them up with deceptive ease. Perhaps the Diplomatic Service, if only his recent peccadilloes could be concealed, would be one answer. He could certainly charm a bird off a tree. Some remote colony—

'Dear Mrs Pallant, the scissors are mislaid.'

The scissors were communal property and entirely necessary, and Olave got up, her skirts rustling, to discover that she had been sitting on them. Amusement was general, and she made herself smile, thereby resembling a bay mare. The last threads of scratchy greyish comprehensive shirts with long sleeves were duly snipped, the shirts themselves folded for conveyance to graceful naked Africans who would lose them as soon as possible in the bush, and Olave said brightly, in the strident family voice, 'And now, ladies, I believe I may ring for tea to be brought in? It has been a busy and successful afternoon for us all.' One must keep up appearances, denying thereby any spiteful gossip. Any other father would have whacked Ivor stupid.

The bishop had, as it happened, broached the subject with his unregenerate son. 'I should administer a sound thrashing, Ivor, but I gather that you have received them frequently at school without effect or benefit.'

Ivor smiled narrowly; he somewhat resembled a fox-cub. 'I enjoyed it,' he said. 'Some of the fellows have a club that meets once a week in the cellar, and we use whips on each other. It's great fun. It stimulates the—'

The bishop did not want to hear what it stimulated, and raised his hand either for silence or else in blessing. It had at times occurred to him to wonder why the decrees of Providence, which of course are inscrutable, had seen fit to visit him with a son who increasingly resembled, in looks and, evidently, in nature, the Apollo of Veii. Of all the versions of the various Apollos – Phoebus, Athenon, the Cretan, the Delphic, the Nomion born in Arcadia – Horace Pallant chiefly remembered seeing in Tuscany, in youth on the briefly revived Grand Tour during the fragile peace with France, the terrible archaic smile of the Etruscan god, and the slightly oblique eyes which looked at him now without shame – evidently the boy felt none – from beneath Ivor's centrally sited peak of red hair. That colouring had never been in the family, but it was impossible to picture Olave as straying in any fashion from the path of virtue. It was simply the will of God that he and Olave should have a cross of the kind to carry; after all, in most ways they were fortunate.

Nevertheless he himself was deeply shamed by the letter he had received from Ivor's late headmaster, a fellow-cleric. It was to the effect that Horace's only son had predilections which made him unfit to associate with other boys, particularly the younger ones. He must be returned to the vigilance of his parents, as there seemed no way of bringing him to deprecate himself.

The bishop had an idea. 'It occurs to me, then, that the only thing to do, as chastisement has no effect on you, is to cut off your allowance until you can control your own conduct.'

'I'll borrow. Any of the old girls here will lend me money, and it will go all round the diocese that you're mean.'

The smile was undiminished, the confidence unshaken. The bishop, generally a mild man, felt his blood rise.

'In that case I shall be forced to insert a notice in the newspapers to the effect that I will not be responsible for any debts you may incur.'

'Mama wouldn't let you, and it's her money.'

Ivor laughed, revealing sharp white teeth, a young animal's. 'Get out of my sight,' said the bishop testily. When Ivor had gone he rested his head on his hands. He was at a loss to know how to deal with such a son. Christian fortitude demanded that he should not inflict the like burden on a tutor, but educate the boy himself. Perhaps a study of the classics would at least interest Ivor.

An unclouded memory suddenly came to console the bishop. It was from Tuscany, like the Apollo, but this was the goddess of love, Aphrodite, Venus; unearthed at that time in one of the recent excavations at Tarquinia. She had been lying with her forearm bent over a couch, her other arm broken off at the wrist, perhaps once having toyed with a mirror. The statue had been very old, seventh century B.C. Pallant had been entranced by the sight of her perfect breasts; whoever had carved, in that archaic age, the red obedient stone had had a peerless model. Her eyes had been more direct than the oblique gaze of the Apollo. Hadn't there been some scandal in the time of the old gods, an affair between the goddess of love, married, out of Jove's revenge, to the lame Vulcan, and caught making love instead with Mars? Apollo had played traitor, and had never been forgiven. The old gods were lascivious, unfit for the thoughts of a churchman to dwell on; no doubt that was why he thought of them by their Roman names; the gods of Rome were, on the whole, concerned with virtue.

Pallant himself had sad thoughts of Rome. In the year of his tour, being still a young man, he had seen a procession entering a church. It was made up of creatures with smooth disillusioned faces, no longer young. They were castrati, whose voices no longer earned them a living and who carried bottles in which their severed parts had been kept from the beginning, for this ultimate purpose, in order that they might present the whole of themselves as candidates for the priesthood, as an alternative to starving in old age. The sight had almost unmanned Pallant; and had made him determine to support the policy of the Church of England in permitting celibacy to be voluntary. He decided then to look about him for the right wife, and to lead the life of a full man as well as a churchman.

It hadn't happened at once, although he had continued in theory to oppose Hildebrandine notions. Over the years as they passed, he had obtained preferment by devotion to duty in all ways; reading, preaching, succouring the poor and afflicted in cities and in the countryside, as Christ had done; expounding theology later to students, by which time, as much to set an example as for any other reason, he had married Olave Masterson, by then thirty-three. He could not, for he was honest with himself, say that he was unattracted by the prospect of money from old Aaron; it would be employed for charitable purposes; also, Olave was a good manager. If only she had had a vestige of beauty! However one could not have everything; and he himself was no longer young by then. The prospect of a coming child had given him surprised pleasure; then, afterwards, nothing but pain. Often he thought, for consolation, of the goddess of love ftom Tarquinia. He had, instead, Apollo in cruel mood, daily before his eyes.

He turned to prayer, as was his wont; and an answer was sent. He must undertake the boy's education himself, and see if gentleness would prevail. Meantime, he sat here with his head in his hands. He would never again set eyes on Aphrodite. He reproached himself for a certain lingering frivolity.

27

*

Aaron Masterson received a letter from his lawyers about then. It contained the news of Nathan Bevan's death. Contained inside was a sealed envelope, which the dead man had ordered to be delivered to him unopened. Its date was some years back. Nathan had evidently assumed that he, Aaron, would live the longer of the two. He opened the letter now with fingers that did not tremble and which were still strong, a potter's who could mould clay.

> *My dear Aaron,*
>
> *This will not reach you till I am dead. If I still lived, you would come and kill me; and despite everything I value my life even though I have been blind for many years. Other senses perfect themselves, and since Sophy died I require no company except the man's to whom I shall dictate this letter.*
>
> *Sophy did not die at the time you supposed. I will relate the whole of this matter from the beginning, as what lies in our hearts is the cause of sin. I am aware of my own, and must live with the memory of it.*
>
> *From the beginning I loved two people, Sophy my sister and yourself. When it became clear that the two of you had eyes only for one another, I was jealous on account of you both. You had no eyes at that time for me, your friend. Moreover, though Sophy was my sister I craved her body. You know the little figure I made later on out of Saxon clay. That was after she was dead; but I did not need to have her before me to remember every curve and line. I gave you the figure because I could no longer bear to look at it, and would have smashed it in self-reproach.*
>
> *You and Sophy plighted your troth still young. I was some years older. Not long after, I took her up to the attics of our house on some*

excuse, and ravished her. I remember how bitterly she wept, and reproached me because you would not find her a virgin. I used the excuse to persuade our parents to compel her into the marriage with Southern, whom she did not love. I did not, therefore, have to envy him; and you would never have her maidenhead. It was the sin of David's son Amnon with his sister Tamar, and since then I have known myself accursed; no doubt the Lord has sent me blindness as a punishment. When one is damned, all things fall into place. I could damn myself no further and have continued down my own pathway into hell. Sophy is in heaven. From the beginning, she was innocent.

When Southern found out on the wedding night that she was not a virgin, he beat her severely. He continued to do this and to be suspicious of her all through the course of the marriage. As you recall, in the end she ran to you. I could not endure the thought of you together thereafter, any more than at first. Day after day I persuaded Sophy of her sin, and made her return to Southern. He beat her again, but not so hard that she died of it, as I caused you to believe. That time she did not dare go back to you, for he would have followed her. Instead, she came to me. I was about to leave for Germany, as you remember, and I hid her and told her that she might accompany me on condition that we lived there as man and wife, being unknown and having no resemblance to one another. So badly bruised and fearful was she that she agreed, though not willingly. I took her, veiled, out of the country, and meantime had written an unsigned letter to the police. It said Southern's wife could not be found, that she had been heard crying out at his beatings, and that he might well have destroyed her body in one of the kilns after beating her to death. I heard later that they found a bloodstained riding-crop in his house; that was fortunate, and supported my story. Being a taciturn man he would say nothing in his own defence, stubbornly refusing to answer questions. I had no regrets when they hanged him.

We lived near Meissen together, Sophy and I, as man and wife. I found work in the factory, learning a great deal about the higher firing temperatures needed for porcelain clay. As some compensation to you, I have helped to make you rich by it. I used to leave Sophy, who spoke no German, in charge of a woman with whom she could not exchange words. I desired to become all in all to her. I did not permit her to leave the house unless accompanied by me. One day she told me she was with child. She was herself uncertain whether it was mine or yours, and again I was engulfed with jealousy.

It will never be known who was the child's father. Sophy went into labour, perhaps prematurely or else not; but in any case she died at the birth. The child was a daughter, and had she been born of incest the tale goes that she would have resembled an ape. She did not, though she had none of her mother's beauty. I called her Hannah, and brought her home. I had by then burned Sophy in the great kiln at Meissen, as is not permitted here yet by law. I collected the ashes and later used them as an ingredient in the glaze of the little figure I had made of her; there was enough left also to glaze a bowl. I have it here and take my food from it always. No one else may use it, and I live alone here except for the man who tends me, and who is writing this letter.

The child Hannah I took up to the north parts, where the sect may be found to which I and my parents belonged. They are strict, and I knew would rear the child strictly, also choose her a husband in proper course from among themselves. I used to send money for her keep, and meantime had returned to work with yourself, bringing with me all I had learned at Meissen. It was then I heard the details of Southern's hanging, which greatly pleased me.

Hannah Bevan – I gave her my name – was married in the north to a man somewhat older, but of upright nature. He fathered a daughter on her, who by now is eight years old. They have called her Tabitha, which means a gazelle, and may also mean that she has beauty. I do not know, for I have never seen her with my eyes, though she is familiar to me and comes each day.

Hannah's husband died and she married a second time, then died herself. I do not greatly like the man, who is now her widower. I sought the solitude of these northern places again at last, and will meet death here. It troubles me that her stepfather will be in charge of Tabitha when she is older. I would ask you, remembering your feeling for her grandmother, to become her guardian. I have left directions accordingly, and no doubt the stepfather will bring her to you himself, as it is my wish. Tabitha is an affectionate child, too much so for her own good She is quick to learn most things.

I will leave you now, my old friend and rival. I have a pain in my vitals, and not long to live. What I have I have left in trust for Tabitha. She hardly remembers her mother, who died when she was small.

The rest is in your hands, your strong potter's hands. Clay is like flesh, to be moulded. We grew rich together, but I have done what I could to expiate my sin by giving generously to the funds of the community here, who distribute them to charity after maintaining themselves in simple fashion. God may partly forgive my sin regarding Sophy, or else consign me to everlasting flames. I shall soon know. The man who is writing this letter is sworn to secrecy, and when I am dead will break the glazed bowl and place it in my coffin to be buried with me.

> *Your friend, despite everything that has been,*
> *Nathan Bevan*

At first, Aaron's mind had remained suspended, then it began to turn slowly, a potter's wheel when someone has started slowly to kick. Tears began to run down his furrowed cheeks. He was aware of savage anger that Sophy had been alive while he was mourning her as dead. All the time she had been in thrall to her brother, possessed by him, lain with, fondled, lusted after against her will. That Nathan should have come home in the end, grim and silent as always, saying nothing of what had come about, was abominable, unforgivable. Southern's fate was the least of it; the man deserved it. Firing temperatures for kaolin; a new dimension added to the business; and Sophy's ashes enshrined in a receipt for glaze.

He reached out and touched the figurine, knowing now that he touched her bones. A child born perhaps to him, perhaps to her brother; nobody would ever know now. and the girl from the north must come, who meant nothing to him and who had been forced on him; he didn't want to set eyes on her, yet would do so once, then she should go off to school, or else back to the strange sect, whichever seemed preferable. It would, after all, do no harm to see her. Meantime, he knew what he must do to calm his mind; a thing he hadn't done for years. It might make him feel young again, bring back the time with Sophy. He would make his way down to the workroom, and throw a pot.

It was night outside by then, with the stars obscured by thick smoke emitted by the ever-burning kilns. He could see their glowing bases in the darkness, and the antlike figures that stoked them. Moving slowly, he groped his way out and down to the wheel-room, seeing the lidded bins in place, full of ready wedged clay. He briefly remembered the young man George, for whom he had had a feeling which by now baffled him. George had kept the clay from drying out. which could happen quickly in summer. He—

Better not to think of it. Aaron flung on a potter's slop, opened a bin and, from habit, wedged the clay again, one could never be too certain. The strong fists made, once more, his own ox-head, the familiar twisting afterwards to get rid of air. Till that was done, clay wasn't personal.

Satisfied at last, he carried the doubly wedged lump to a wheel, gave a side-kick to the latter and, watching it begin to turn, cast the clay on its moving surface. He continued to kick, seeing the wheel increase in speed, fashioning, with the familiar potter's grip, a rising cylinder. A single wall-lamp, all they left burning at night, threw his monstrous shadow on the wall. He completed a pot with vigour, feeling the anger leave him and find a home in the shaped clay. There were standpipes in which to dip one's hands continuously in water. Pots, plates, cups, jugs; he hadn't the desire tonight to add handles and a spout, merely to throw and shape. When the pot was finished, whatever it was, he trimmed it off with a knife and put it up on the shelf used for drying greenware. He threw two more, then felt tired; there was no point in continuing tonight. They could think what they liked in the morning, recognising the master's touch. It wouldn't be ready for firing for three weeks, and in three weeks he might well be dead. He had familiarised himself with the thought of death over recent years; it would come as a friend, a friend like Nathan? Now he was angry again; he shouldn't have cast his thoughts backwards.

He rinsed his hands, seeing clay left under the rims of the nails, as in old days. He took off the potter's slop, hung it on its hook, and made his way stiffly upstairs again, though not to bed. Instead he went to his writing-desk, which Margaret called an escritoire, and wrote a letter to the address Nathan had given. *Bring the child to me.*

33

He rang then for a servant, who came, blinking sleep from his eyes; it was by then the middle of the night. 'Get this to the post straight away,' said Masterson. 'I want it to go first thing in the morning. Take a lantern.'

He stood at the window to make sure he was obeyed, seeing the swaying yellow lantern go off in the man's hand. They needn't think they could disobey him nowadays because he was old. Nobody had made a fool of him since Nathan took Sophy away; and nobody would again.

He betook himself to bed then, by now near morning. Margaret was quietly asleep in the next room; for some years he'd preferred total solitude. He lay awake and thought of the child's coming. A sight of her, one way or the other, might be enough.

3

'THIS is Tabitha Bevan. You wanted her brought.'

The voice was unsociable, as though affability was not permitted. The man who spoke had not removed his hat, and a pair of pale eyes stared out from beneath its brim, with at the back of them the mad, inevitable spark of the dedicated sectarian. Masterson disliked the breed, heard himself ask why the child's name was still Bevan and was told that the habit was to maintain the mother's. Aaron stared at the child. She might be eight or nine years old. It was difficult to tell, as she was swathed in ugly clothing; a shawl on her shoulders, her feet in clogs, and on her head a cambric cap concealing her hair. Brown eyes stared back, beseechingly. He addressed Hannah's widower without looking at him again.

'You may leave her with me. If you go downstairs they will give you something to eat, and money to refund your journey.'

'I myself do not need money, but it will be paid into the community for the relief of deserving cases.'

The unctuousness repelled Aaron and he was glad the man had gone, wondering if the late Hannah's second choice had been her own or her father's. When they were alone he beckoned the little girl to him, and pulled off her cap. A mass of golden hair tumbled out, to his delight. He began to play with it, setting her on his knee. He sent for one of the housemaids.

'Take off these clothes,' he said. The servant looked disapproving, as far as she dared. It was a long time since things of the kind had been whispered about the old man. She hadn't had any trouble with him herself; he was supposed to be past it. She ventured to ask if it was quite proper to undress the little girl. Meantime, their owner had kicked her own clogs off. They rattled to the floor, leaving small feet in woollen stockings. Aaron laughed.

'Then let us be improper. Sophy, let her undress you. I want to see you without any clothes at all.'

'I'm Tabitha.'

'No, I think you are Sophy. Let us see.' He was filled, for the first time in years, with a sense of joy and expectation. The eyes surveyed him again between dark-gold lashes; they were very slightly different from those he remembered, having green specks like moss-agate. It was as if she was asserting her separate identity; otherwise, she was Sophy over again.

She allowed the servant to do as she had been bidden, then Aaron took her once more on his knee. The new Sophy didn't seem disturbed while he fondled her smooth ivory limbs. Her former name had meant a gazelle; he was surprised that the graceless sect should have thought of it.

The body was still a child's; that would change, and he hoped to live to see the flat breasts grow; meantime, with the servant gone off with the clothes to burn them, his strong hands stroked, caressed, pried. The little tight virginity, necessary for marriage, was still present; neither Nathan, purveyor of incest, nor the step-father had penetrated her. Her hands and feet were beautiful, the nails like shells. He kissed her, and the child put up with it;

his kisses were like cold india-rubber, she decided, but he seemed kind. What he was doing wasn't as bad as what her stepfather had taken to lately, on the night before meetings when God inspired him with long prayers that went on and on. He had taken to sending for her out of bed, then would make her bend over the kitchen table and pull her nightgown up, while he took off the leather belt he wore. When he'd finished using it on her she often couldn't sit down next day. He called it chastising her for her own good. It wasn't as if she had done anything wrong in particular; it was as though he was getting rid of something inside himself he knew oughtn't to be there. It hadn't used to happen before her mother died.

At meetings, she had often had to stand to listen to the prayers, and otherwise everyone kept silence. Everyone knew why she was standing, with her eyes and nose red with crying: the girls looked pleased, and she would see some of the boys grin who'd asked her now and again to let them kiss her. Now, this old man was kissing her anyway. She was glad to be away from the school where her stepfather taught, although she'd learnt a lot, having been made to.

She heard the sound of the cob riding off on which they'd come, with the side-saddle on which she'd sat knocking empty against the cob's flanks. The side-saddle had been made of wood, safe but not comfortable. She said something about it; it was a relief to be able to speak without being silenced.

'You shall have a pony of your own,' promised Aaron Masterson.

Margaret, informed by the shocked housemaid of events, came in shortly, carrying a clean linen chemise. 'At least put this on her,' she said. It really would not do to kiss and fondle a naked little girl, even so young. He was still busy caressing the child, and raised his head only briefly.

'Very well, put the damned thing on,' he said. 'You will send to London at once for pretty clothes, as you used to do for the girls.' He pictured the clothes, and Sophy in them; puff-sleeved dresses, so that he could stroke her bare arms; frilly petticoats and drawers, bonnets, muffs, pelisses for when it was cold; everything in fashion. 'We'll turn you out finely, eh, Sophy?' Only he and she would know what was underneath, now and later.

Margaret meanwhile had put the chemise on the child, who stood passive. 'Come with me to have something to eat after your journey,' said Margaret firmly. She had endured various situations in the course of her marriage, after all. It was possible the old man meant well enough.

The second Sophy thereafter lacked for nothing. Not only was she bought pretty clothes she could never have imagined, velvet for winter, sprigged muslin for summer, bonnets to frame her face with its golden curls allowed to show, slippers and white lace stockings held up with embroidered garters; a sealskin muff and matching pelisse; a little purse to hold inside with pocket-money: and the pony. Besides all this there was a dancing-master and French governess, and Mr Masterson used to come in while they were chattering in French, or when she was learning the cotillion and the waltz. She liked that; there hadn't been anything of the kind where she had come from. When she was older, Mr Masterson – he liked her to call him Grandfather Aaron by then, however, in the same way as the old blind man in the north had been Grandfather Nathan – said that when she was older, she was to have a London season and be presented to the Queen, in a long train and feathers. 'If my elder daughter won't do it, we'll hire a marchioness.' Talking in French, singing in German with the music-master, who said she had a promising voice; nothing was left undone to turn her into a finished young lady. Time passed quickly, and suddenly she was no longer a child; and every day the old master potter would send for her, set her on his knee and fondle and kiss her. She became used to it; after all he didn't use a leather belt. She had been brought up to silence, and didn't talk much except at French lessons; once Grandfather Aaron asked her about her mother, and what she had looked like.

'Not like me. She was dark.' Both he and Nathan had been dark young men; it might be either, he decided, and in any case it didn't matter. He had Sophy again. Now that the eccentric conditions in which she had earlier been reared were gone, she began to show her true nature; trusting, impulsive, affectionate. Even Margaret began to be fond of her, but was allowed little say in her upbringing. Aaron saw to that himself, it was like glazing a finished pot; the best he had ever thrown. The analogy amused him.

Sophy never was presented to the Queen in a train and feathers, as Aaron died when she was fourteen years old. He had already made his will, and expressed in it the wish that his descendants should inherit the blood of the earlier Sophy, her grandmother. This accounted for what were afterwards considered eccentric conditions, but there was no doubt that Aaron Masterson had been of sound mind even on his deathbed.

On that occasion, all his illegitimate sons had been called to the bedside, and Margaret was asked to bring Sophy in. She came, in a white dress, with her hair scooped up in a shining knot on top of her head; lately it had grown long enough to reach her knees, and though beautiful was inconvenient. However the dying man instructed her to let it down.

'I want to die with your hair like a veil over my face,' he whispered. He was propped up on pillows for easier breathing, but the breaths by now were rasping, his voice laboured. Sophy recalled how kind he had always been to her, let down her soft hair and spread it, at the same time leaning over to give him a kiss.

He reached out a hand, and stroked the new young slender curve of her breast, his eyes fading and contented. 'All of my sons here are married, and mostly breed daughters,' he murmured. 'You must bear a son to the husband of your choice; it's all written down. You won't want for bite and sup in the meantime, Sophy, Aphrodite. Don't forget me, I'm going now. Give me your hand.'

She gave him her small hand, and let him breathe the scent of her hair; one moment he was alive, the next a shell. The grip on her hand did not lessen and they had to prise it away. She heard Margaret Masterson's voice.

'Pin up your hair again, Sophy. My husband is dead.' She gestured the rest to leave, and herself closed the curtains, She had shown, and had probably felt, no conventional grief.

Sophy herself was glad he'd said that about bite and sup, as otherwise she might not have been certain what was to happen to her. She certainly didn't want to go back to her stepfather and the life she had left behind; how narrow and impossible it seemed now! She had learned all kinds of things about the world; perhaps she could become a governess. She kept her usual silence on that matter, looking down at last on the old master potter's square-jawed face in its coffin. The lines had been

smoothed from it and he looked, despite the grey hair and bald-
ing forehead, much as he must have done when her grandmother Sophy – he'd told her about that by now – had loved him;
almost godlike. Otherwise, he had two daughters, one married to
a lord and the other to a bishop. They would be here for the
funeral. He'd called her Aphrodite when he was dying. She
would remember that.

The funeral was attended only by men, as was customary. After
the departure of what seemed like a forest of tall black chimney
hats, the women of the family were left alone.

For some time there was silence in the room, partly out of
respect for the deceased but also, because nobody could think of
anything to say. Margaret wore her weeds and weepers, and was
trying not to look as relieved as she felt. She had done her duty
as far as might be, and should now be able to look forward to a
reasonable jointure. Her daughter and stepdaughter, Clara and
Olave, who seldom met in the ordinary way, sat side by side looking down their noses. They had never had much in common in
the first place, and had had handsome marriage-portions settled
upon them in the second. In other words, they didn't hope for
much now.

Sophy sat in her black mourning dress, feeling an irrepressible
desire to sing, dance, laugh, or whistle, precisely because none of
them were allowed. In proper mourning, nothing of the kind
could be done for a year. In a year, she'd be fifteen. It wasn't, as
Grandfather Aaron would himself have said, much of a compliment to the dead to have to go about with long faces, as if they'd
gone decidedly downwards instead of upwards. There was no
reason why God should want to punish Grandfather. He had
bought her a great many pretty dresses, had never been anything

41

but kind, and the cold rubbery kisses and fondlings had pleased him and had had to be put up with. She was glad now that she hadn't wriggled away, that she had contented him in such ways; they seemed to be all he asked. She hadn't shed tears or felt sad when she saw him lying in his coffin; he was somewhere else, and she hoped he was happy.

The lord and the bishop had reacted in their separate ways to news of the decease, which moved neither of them greatly; after all it was a considerable age to reach. The bishop had agreed to take the funeral service, but thereafter had to attend a convocation in London. Lord Tenterdowne had an engagement there also, an auction of rare books from a famous collection. Both drove off, therefore, without waiting to hear the will read. It was improbable that either of them would benefit; the church had been filled, in two rows in front, with Aaron Masterson's illegitimate sons, mostly resembling him to an extent which caused one to feel as if confronted by tables of logarithms or a hatching out of frog's eggs. Sons' wives and wives' sons waited to hear the lawyer read out the old reprobate's last intentions; and the bishop, in his unworldly way, hardly by now recalled a long-legged girl seated among the rest in the drawing-room. He was more greatly exercised, as usual, over Ivor, whose behaviour in general was enough to turn his father's grey hairs white. There was a pagan streak in the inheritance, and surely, like the red hair, not from his own side; old Aaron's wish to be burned after death in one of his own kilns rather than let the worms get him was no doubt after the manner of the ancients, but not yet legal in Britain. Worms, mused the bishop, got us all in the end, or all that was mortal; the rest was a matter for Divine Providence. It would be comforting to meet his fellow-bishops at the convocation, and be reassured in his faith.

Tenterdowne was thinking differently, and not altogether of first editions. He had done more than glimpse Sophy, and had seen in her the perfect Cranach, though still unripe. Without lasciviousness – he was after all an aesthete rather than a lecher, he told himself – he decided to tell Clara to bring the girl to Lawley for a long visit. The girl had, when all was said, been old Aaron's ward, though nobody seemed quite certain who she was or where she came from. Something should be done by somebody; and she would be safer out of the reach of that unspeakable young monster, Ivor Pallant.

Neither of the two had heard, or would hear till their wives told them at home, of the terms of Aaron Masterson's will. Madeira had been served in small glasses before the reading of the document itself, and afterwards Margaret sat outraged, wondering if the wine had affected her hearing. She was incredulous. She had been left a sum, certainly, which would enable her to live in decency, but it wasn't lush. Neither had the illegitimate sons profited greatly, having their positions in the firm already assured. Everything, except for a few small legacies to favourite old servants – everything, the pottery and gravel refinery and subsidiaries and the shares in flax and cotton, had gone to that golden-haired miss who wasn't even a relation, and had come out of nowhere only three years ago, or was it longer than that? Yes, it must be four or five; time had gone quickly. Margaret Masterson sat plum-faced with resentment between her weepers, which fortunately obscured her complexion. The girl's guardians were to be the bishop and Lord Tenterdowne, and that wasn't all. The interest on endowments was to be Sophy Bevan's, but the whole was eventually to go to a son she should bear either to Ivor

Pallant or to Charley, Clara's son, whichever she preferred as a husband. The whole arrangement was iniquitous, so much so that perhaps a legal enquiry should be made to try to overturn it. Already dear Clara and dear Olave were glaring fiercely at one another, as if determined on the part of each to become the heiress's mother-in-law. It was enough to split a family in two for generations, and no doubt Aaron had entertained himself with exactly such a prospect. He had always been unreasonable.

'I think, dear Clara, that as you are less occupied than I, it would be fitting if you were to take charge of the little heiress first,' grated Olave Pallant. As usual, there was method in her every utterance, and the fact that was that she hoped the constant sight of lumpish Charley would induce young Sophy to prefer the very idea of anybody else; and if in the course of the years Ivor could be improved in manners and morals to match his undoubted good looks, there was no doubt as to who would become the eventual son's father. Slim as a young god, but unfortunately with a god's propensities, Ivor was a sight to set any young woman's heart beating faster; that was, until they became acquainted.

Clara agreed, with an eye to the main chance also. Charley might not be much to look at, but he had an affectionate nature and would no doubt make a faithful husband. If the two young people got to know one another by sharing the tutor daily, the excellences of Charley's disposition could not fail to become manifest. Ivor's undoubted looks were, on the other hand, a snare and a delusion. Further probabilities escaped Clara, who could not think for long about any subject except her husband.

Sophy chose Lawley at once. The reason wasn't that, in the time before the men returned from Grandfather's funeral, Ivor Pallant had contrived to nip and pinch her, hoping to make her squeal because they had been told to make no noise. She had taken refuge behind Charley's solid form and put her arms round his neck for protection. Charley had liked it, and had fended off Ivor. That however was nothing to do with Sophy's decision; she could after all kick Ivor in a certain place when there wasn't company. No; the reason for choosing Lawley in which to live meantime had been the brief and peerless sight, before he went off to the funeral, of Lord Tenterdowne, Clara's husband. He was the handsomest man Sophy had ever seen in her life.

She announced at once that she would marry Charley. 'There is no haste for a decision till you are of suitable age,' said Margaret absently. Now everything was over she was looking forward in any case to going to live at Scarborough, for some bracing sea air away from the eternal kilns.

Bowling along in the carriage back to Lawley, young Charley Twining – he would be Tenterdowne in time – knew he was in love. The sensation of Sophy's soft young arms sliding round his neck had been the first sign of open affection he ever recalled. He knew he was too fat, and not clever; but he would meet her every wish all his days, if allowed to. He had never imagined anyone as beautiful; and having heard and partly understood the terms of the will, prayed devoutly that he would be the one she'd choose in the end. Perhaps he'd have got thinner by then. He gazed at Sophy where she sat beside Mama in her bombazine, opposite him in the carriage so that he himself had had to be placed with his back to the horses. This was chivalrous, but it made him feel sick. He prayed again that he wouldn't be sick in front of Sophy. He hadn't, come to think of it, known any girls before. How exquisite she was, like an ivory figurine with gold hair! It strayed bewitchingly from below her black mourning-bonnet, and the tiny hands clasped lately about his neck were hidden by now in her muff.

Poor Charley made numerous resolutions about himself; he must stop being so much afraid of horses, it irritated Papa. He must learn to ride properly, so as to be able to escort Sophy at a gallop across the park. He must learn to be clever at cards, and understand what went on in the great world, and read a great deal so as to make intelligent talk instead of, as at present, merely agreeing with what everyone else was saying for the sake of being left in peace. His cousin Ivor, on the other hand, didn't have to say a word, merely standing looking scornful beneath his peaked devil's eyebrows and keeping his arms folded in front of his chest. Charley decided to try that when he had access to a long glass, but sadly feared it would make his stomach bulge even more than it did now. His stomach – ugh—

'If you are about to be sick, Charley, pray rap on the window,' said his mother without compassion.

Afterwards, humiliated beyond belief, he climbed back into the carriage. Sophy smiled lovingly. 'Does it feel better now?' she asked. She didn't seem to be disgusted by his late performance. Life was again full of hope. She'd seen him at his worst, so things could only get better. He hoped she would decide to stay at Lawley for ever.

4

LORD Tenterdowne had a number of reasons for breakfasting
alone by habit. Firstly he disliked saying anything to anyone
before half past nine, and Clara had been brought up to make
polite conversation. Secondly, the sight of his wife and his heir,
both shovelling buttered eggs and toast into their respective
mouths with gusto, was too much for a man of sensibility; Lord
Byron, after all and for similar reasons, had arranged to eat sepa-
rately during the brief course of his own marriage.

The third reason was the earl, making the most of devilled
kidneys but grumbling forever about how his five wits had gone
long ago and he couldn't see. Nevertheless he had seen enough
to be able to remark that Miss Sophy was a damn' fine gel. She
had been with them now three weeks, and shared lessons had
become for Charley an Eden of delight. Tenterdowne had modified his initial outlook on learning the terms of Aaron's will and
that Charley was in the marriage stakes: he had a heart somewhere within a cold protective covering, and didn't want to queer
his son's pitch by aesthetic experiments.

He stayed in his room, therefore, eating absently and recalling
the pleasant sight of the sun shining yesterday on Sophy's golden
hair, and the whisking of her skirts as she ran upstairs past him.

47

Tenterdowne poured himself more coffee, reflecting and remembering; and at this point there came a timid scratching at the door.

It was the tutor, who regretted disturbing his lordship so early. He was a small man with an uncertain face and manner. He had a moderate degree in classics from Cambridge, not as good as it might have been because of natural diffidence. He had been recommended to Tenterdowne by a fellow-bibliophile, who said so gentle a creature might get the best out of poor Charley. The man had been here now two years, and had at least got on with his not very enviable task with the minimum of trouble.

It was, he ventured to say now, about Master Charley that he had come. The young gentleman no longer paid full attention to what anyone said, being too greatly occupied with gazing at Miss Sophy. She herself, on the other hand, outstripped poor Charley in every way, and, apart from already chattering French like a native, seemed to have a grasp of most other subjects except mathematics, which in her case continued weak. That, however – the tutor smirked – was the privilege of young ladies, who turned it to account.

'What do you want me to do about it?' put in Tenterdowne without warmth. It was evident the fellow laboured under a stronger emotion that he would admit. Charley's inattention could have been dealt with in the ordinary way; and no doubt the tutor himself found Sophy's presence disturbing. The thought diverted Tenterdowne and at the same time, roused his sympathy. 'If,' he heard the poor tutor stammer, 'your lordship – this may be an impertinence – would care to undertake, even for a part of each day, her instruction, even perhaps allowing her to read in the library—'. He reiterated that perhaps he ought not to have made a suggestion of the kind, and blushed abjectly.

48

Well, Tenterdowne decided, nobody could blame *him* for the notion. He agreed to relieve the tutor of his torment in afternoons. After the man had gone he divested himself of his dressing-gown, had himself shaved and put on riding-clothes. Attired thus, he took himself out to inspect the coverts and to obtain some fresh air and exercise; it was a mistake to sit all day over books, tempting as the life had proved. On the way back he encountered his father, driving, as the latter frequently did, to visit the home farm, where he liked to scratch the pigs' backs from the low-swung pony trap and talk to them in the way pigs understand. He remarked again that Miss Sophy was a fine piece, and that the late Masterson had known what he was doin' in puttin' her on the market.

It was a limited market, as Tenterdowne already knew; either Charley or the bishop's son. From all he had seen of young Ivor at brief, because necessary, family exchanges, looks might tell. Again, he had no wish to make matters more difficult for Charley than they already were. He would undertake Miss Sophy in afternoons, and keep the occasions strictly proper, with no overtones.

He reckoned without nature, and the young lady.

It had been decided that the new arrangements should begin on Monday. On the previous day, after church, Tenterdowne happened to be standing near his window and could see, below in the park, his son and Sophy out riding. Sophy was a natural rider, with good hands and a better seat; her supple dark-clad figure reminded him of some enchanted being which was half mount, half girl; a female centaur, but with pervasive beauty. It gave him pleasure to watch her curvet and canter. Charley, on the other hand, rode like a sack of coal. He would never be a good horseman, and the father in some despair wondered if his son could ever be good at anything; most things had been tried. While Sophy veered and increased speed divinely, in the end riding off at the full gallop, Charley plodded along, hardly daring to rise to the trot. Tenterdowne saw Sophy come back at last, flushed and laughing, to her laggard lover. It was evident that she had patience with him.

Later that afternoon Tenterdowne met her, still untidy from the ride, her hair escaping in bright ringlets from the confines of the net, having pulled off her riding-hat. It occurred to him that he had never seen her look more beautiful. *A sweet disorder in the dress.* Who had written that? He should know at once, but his wits deserted him. He hardly heard what Sophy was saying: something about his son.

'Poor Charley is not very well. He says it hurts him to turn his neck. He has gone back to bed, and they've sent for the doctor.'

How sweet her voice was, like chiming silver bells! He watched her go, and felt deprived of her company. This would never do. He must discipline himself, as her preceptor, not to give way to such feelings. It was a simple matter of strictness with himself and her. He was, at least, forewarned of the necessity.

It turned out that the Honourable Charley Twining had mumps. 'I've had them,' said Sophy to Charley's father. So had he; they must have been brought into the house by one of the servants from a day off. It was tiresome, Clara said; the whole house would be infected, and there could be no callers.

To spare the afflicted tutor from having to endure her sole company, Tenterdowne decided that it was his clear duty to take Sophy riding in the mornings. He gave the man three weeks' leave of absence till everyone should be recovered. In afternoons, he had arranged to read with Sophy, as already expected.

After their first ride together – it had been enjoyable, he admitted – he sat reading in the library, determined to make no special matter of her arrival. She came in then, having changed into a summer gown of fluid muslin, with a broad ribbon sash tied in a bow at the back, outlining her slim waist. Her hair was caught up, as usual these days, in the great knot of gold on top of her head, but little tendrils strayed on her white neck, seen closely when he instructed her to choose a book for herself from the shelves. 'You may choose whatever you wish,' he said impersonally, indicating where the French literature was arranged, she might like that; he then forced himself to return to his own reading, and found that he could not concentrate on it. Suddenly he resolved, savagely, to sketch Sophy as she read; in his young days he had made a pastime of it, and there were pencils in a drawer. She was still standing with her back turned, making her choice, when Tenterdowne achieved the first sketch. It would be something to keep; her bent neck, the soft straying tendril, the folds of her dress, the tied bow.

'You may dispose yourself comfortably,' he told her, still the preceptor, but he had not anticipated that she would do anything but sit down. There was a *chaise-longue* nearby, and Sophy proceeded to dispose herself, stretching out her graceful limbs, one forearm bent across her body, the other hand holding a light book. Tenterdowne was less well acquainted than his brother-in-law the bishop with Etruscan goddesses, but he had seen the Elgin Marbles in London, also the Canova statue, purchased by the Duke of Devonshire, of Napoleon's beautiful naked sister, Princess Pauline Borghese. The Princess, one understood, had had ugly ears and kept them covered. Sophy's ears were, on the other hand, delectable as little blossoms, set high above her long neck. Below, her breasts were no longer

51

purely Cranach. Tenterdowne heard his voice grow thick.

'What are you reading?' he made himself say. He was being carried away on a wave of the sea; he recalled that the goddess Aphrodite had arrived, borne on a sea-shell, on the shores of Cythera, having been unaccountably fashioned out of foam.

He was however able to say, when it turned out to be *Les Liaisons Dangereuses*, 'That is not for you,' and went over and took the book firmly from her; he should of course have selected her reading. Sophy gazed up at him with her moss-agate eyes, her body retaining the unashamed grace of a young animal. Evidently she had no self-consciousness, and certainly no shame.

'I've read it already,' she said. 'I wanted to refresh my vocabulary.'

He replaced the book on the shelves without comment, and found something more suitable; a volume of early English poetry. 'Read one or two of these to yourself, then select one to recite to me aloud,' he told her. Irresistibly, he made a second sketch while she read. This time he found that he had conveyed the lines of her body as if she wore no clothes. It had not been his intention, and the result shocked him slightly. It was as if the chilly carapace in which he had enfolded himself since his marriage was already cracking, making him behave irresponsibly. He must stay firmly within it, and remember poor Charley.

Presently, having sketched in a line or two of clothing as well as it might now be done, he heard her silvery voice read out a poem he had long forgotten; Ben Jonson's *Let it not your wonder move*. He tried to think that it was accidental that she had chosen one which made it clear old men could still love. Old? He was still in his forties. *She shall make the old man young.* No doubt she was remembering her deceased patron Aaron Masterson, his father-in-law, who one understood had been only doubtfully a relation.

First, prepare you to be sorie
That you never knew till now
Either whom to love, or how.

She raised her eyes then, and smiled. Was she doing it on purpose to torment him? He must certainly pass part of the day in some other fashion, either leaving Sophy alone in the library or else asking Clara to be present. The latter prospect however depressed him. He told himself Clara usually had callers in the afternoons, and that such an arrangement would no doubt inconvenience her.

John Tenterdowne continued to ride out with Sophy at his side in the mornings; it seemed safe in the open air. Poor Charley was still in bed, recovering slowly. Sophy herself would visit him first and comfort him, then emerge, charming beyond belief in her riding-habit, its folds disposed gracefully over one arm, her hair hidden beneath the severe tall hat, revealing the delicacy of her facial bones. They would mount and canter, then gallop, through the park, once going as far as the little river, where a deep gully at last formed its natural waterfall among the stones. Sophy exclaimed with delight at first seeing it; she hadn't come as far before. She got down out of the saddle, and in courtesy he could hardly fail to do the same. There was a wooden seat placed ready, where more than one person could sit and survey the foaming water.

'I love it,' said Sophy. 'Let's come here often. Let's come every day.'

To his disturbance she slid then on to his knee, put her arms round his neck and began kissing him, repeatedly and softly.

Sensations rose in Tenterdowne he knew he ought not to feel. He tried to thrust her away.

'Don't pretend you don't like it. Grandfather Aaron used to. He didn't like me to stop.'

Her lips were like rosy velvet; where would all this lead? He clung to the thought of Charley, trapped in bed with mumps.

'I am not your grandfather, but possibly your future father-in-law. Such behaviour is improper.' He put her firmly off his knee: the warm nearness of her flesh still made him remember he was a man. He had allowed himself to forget that over the years, turning to books, to scholarship, to coldness.

She replied, unperturbed, that she was very fond of Charley. 'He's kind, but you're handsome as well, so I love you best.' She began to rub her smooth cheek against his shaven one. 'I love you, I love you, I love you,' she said, still softly, but with determination.

'You are behaving very badly. If this continues, our rides must cease.'

She pouted most adorably. 'All right, let's go back.'

He lifted her without further visible incident into the saddle, and they rode back in silence. He must be Adonis to her Venus, he told himself, must fly from her by every means, or else be lost; even if it ended by becoming a little bloodstained flower, as had happened in the legend.

Sophy continued unperturbed in the library, again choosing her own reading, including Chaucer; and by now, Tenterdowne was aware that even that earthy and entertaining personage could teach her very little she did not already know. At times he found himself almost unable to resist letting her know she was loveable; she knew it anyway. However he resisted further rides to the water, taking her instead to view the home farm and the pigs. 'I've always felt sorry for the Gadarene swine,' remarked Sophy. 'It wasn't their fault.'

Aphrodite, Aphrodite! When she talked so it was harder than ever not to catch her in his arms and kiss her. As it was, the thought of her began to haunt him even in absence.

Clara Tenterdowne was meantime not insensible of the situation. Her own presence was demanded much less often in the library, all else apart. Had it been Olave, she would have insisted on being present for the sake of propriety; it certainly wasn't proper the way the young minx laid herself out on the chaise-longue, as one had noted through the keyhole on more than one occasion. Clara had also, in proper course of investigation during the rides, come across the sketches her husband had made, which confirmed her unease. He had not only outlined the young woman's breasts as though they were totally uncovered, but had actually drawn the unmentionable mystery between her thighs. 'He never drew *me*,' Clara thought resentfully. It was time to act; and one day she sat down and wrote to her sister Olave. It was admitting defeat, but money was not everything; and it was after all most unlikely that Sophy would tempt the bishop. She had matured amazingly since poor Charley took to his bed, however, and he wouldn't be out again quite yet. The doctor was worried, saying Charley should have caught mumps when he was younger. He hadn't explained further, and one hesitated to ask as it was perhaps better not to know.

> *My dearest Olave*
>   *I trust that you, Horace and Ivor are well. We have had a little upset here with* – and she described the mumpish outbreak,

which had also affected some of the servants, but said it was now safely over. *I do think that, that being the case, it would be only right to give dear Sophy an opportunity to become acquainted with Ivor as well as with Charley. She is growing very much attached to him, but after all there is no one else here young enough to be a companion to her.* Clara smiled to herself; that one was subtle. *Would you be kind enough to take her for a little while, perhaps till she has made up her mind? So much money is a heavy responsibility, and Horace will without doubt want to exercise his due share of the girl's guardianship.*

No doubt, after reflection, you will like to let me know of a suitable date to bring Sophy across in the carriage, with a few of her gowns. It will soon be time for her to have others, and you are in a better position to choose them than I.

She remained Olave's ever affectionate sister, Clara Tenterdowne.

5

'I DON'T want to go. I won't go, I won't. I want to stay here with you.'

Sophy's eyes were brimming over with the diamonds of her tears, one of which spilled becomingly down each cheek. They were alone in the library, Clara having broken the news downstairs at luncheon.

Tenterdowne subdued his own torment, which pursued him ever further into sleep. He had dreamt, last night, that he was in the act of possessing her. It was certainly time to separate from the constant temptation of Sophy's presence. He had thought of what to do before hearing of Clara's reply from her sister, which had come by the post. Olave Pallant had naturally urged her sister to bring Sophy without delay.

The Twinings held land in Ireland, where James I had granted a plantation to them among others. The land was supervised by bailiffs, and Tenterdowne knew he should have gone long ago, in the incapacity of his father the earl, to inspect matters. There were too many tales of extortion and neglect, though he believed the present bailiff to be honest. The earl would certainly have no objection to his going to see for himself.

He made himself face Sophy now, downing the desire to take

her in his arms and comfort her. 'I shall not be here,' he said gently. 'I am going for some considerable time to Ireland.' He was uncertain how long: it would take a lifetime to forget her, but she might after all no longer be at Lawley when he returned.

'Take me with you. I want to come with you.'

She flung herself against him, and the touch of her body disturbed him; he made himself put her away.

'That is impossible; neither my wife nor Charley will accompany me. You had best go to the bishop's; there will be diversions there, in the cathedral town.' The scent of her hair was still in his nostrils; how long could he endure?

'You will come back, will you not? Promise you will come back.'

She raised a hand to his cheek; the touch was that of a flower-petal. 'Of course,' he said; it was the truth, after all. Perhaps she would have decided by then to marry young Ivor. That would solve everything.

He watched her go off, shining head bowed, small feet dragging; there would be no reading done that day. He had already sent word for his gear to be packed, but realised that he had not told Clara of his departure, and she should of course have been the first to know. He knew himself to be remiss as a husband.

Informed, Clara firmed her lips. 'That will leave me here alone with Charley and your father,' was all she had to say.

Sophy went later on to say goodbye to Charley, who was up out of bed for the first time and seated languidly in an armchair. His eyes lit up at sight of her.

'I am going away for a little while,' she told him. 'I am going to the bishop, to be made into a good girl.'

That made him laugh, although the thought of losing her had made him sad. It would be dull, he knew, with only the tutor. He

58

hadn't been able to do any of the things he had promised himself he would do, to impress her. 'Come back soon,' he told her; he wasn't good at words, or anything. How beautiful she looked in her velvet travelling-dress, the colour of green grass! Charley gazed in adoration.

'Of course I shall come back,' Sophy said. 'As soon as we're both old enough, we can be married.' It was true, as she'd told his father, that she was very fond of Charley; and marriage to him meant that she could certainly live here rather than there. The cathedral town and its diversions became increasingly unwelcome; but after all Lord Tenterdowne wouldn't be here either. Her mouth drooped.

Charley rose shakily to his feet to bid her farewell. He was flushed with delight that she'd chosen him as a husband, and his head was swimming. The doctor still came daily; he wasn't quite well yet. By the time Sophy returned, especially if they could be married, he would surely feel better. Sophy would help him. She was always kind.

Tenterdowne did not appear to say farewell. Last night, again, he had dreamed of possessing Sophy, her soft flesh under his hands, her mouth on his, her hair a warm scented veil across his face. Then it had come to him that she was really there, had slid into his bed while he slept, had enchanted him to his instant undoing. There had been bliss beyond imagining, while he thought it was still a dream. He recalled murmuring, 'You are Aphrodite, and you were not born of flesh, but of sea-foam; you floated in on a shell.'

Which was dream and which reality he was no longer clear. When he awoke, if indeed he had slept, she had gone, slipping whitely before dawn down the corridors.

59

He waited till he had heard her carriage drive off, then had himself dressed, still dazed, and had gone by late morning, having settled certain matters of business with the earl.

6

THE carriage trundled towards the cathedral town. Inside were Clara, Sophy, and a maid. Had it not been for the latter's presence Clara might, as she put it to herself, have said something. She was still smouldering with resentment at the situation they had left, and the young woman appeared, if one might so put it, *fulfilled*. Such a possibility was of course not to be considered as applying to the austere and scholarly Tenterdowne, off now to carry out his long overdue commitments on the Irish estates. In any case Miss Sophy, with sleepy eyelids and an inexplicable radiance, placed her feet opposite, in unladylike fashion, beside the maid, and announced that she felt like dozing. There was no point, therefore, in attempting conversation.

The baggage, most of it Sophy's, was piled on top. Clara herself did not anticipate staying longer than it took to see her charge safely bestowed and to be certain that the instruction for her confirmation would be as thorough and prolonged as possible. Papa had of course not troubled to see to such things earlier.

One could, however, rely on Olave. Clara looked forward to a long private talk with her sister concerning what could not, in the nature of things, be committed to paper.

Sophy herself was by no means asleep, merely languid with

remembered pleasure. She had given herself utterly, lips, body, mind, heart. Their delight in one another last night in the darkness was a thing to be cherished always, remembered in sadness and echoed in joy. Her virginity – she knew about such things, if only from *Les Liaisons* – had less been rudely broken than, itself, melting readily with an all-pervading desire. (Cécile Volanges in the book had made an unnecessary fuss). Had Tenterdowne been present still, she would have wanted more, and yet more. As it was, she could languish in memory; recall his incomparable presence, his elegant, long fine scholar's hands caressing her with a kind of wonder, as if it was the first time for him as well. It wasn't, of course; he'd had to sleep with old Clara to produce Charley, but that wouldn't have happened, looking at her sour face now, any oftener than it had to. Dear Charley. He seemed a long way away.

She would marry Charley quite soon, perhaps before his father came back from Ireland. Then they could all live together in contentment. It wasn't difficult to please Charley, to bring a smile to his great fat face and a light to his eyes.

They were approaching the first houses now; Sophy felt the road grow smoother, and opened her eyelids. 'You have slept well, I trust,' said Clara, in order to be able to say something. 'We have made fairly good speed, and the weather here continues much the same.'

It was courteous, after all, whatever one's feelings, to indulge in a little conversation. At Lawley, there hardly ever seemed very much, between the earl's pigs and Tenterdowne's library. It would at least be peaceful to be back there without this interloper; one could not, at any time, deny her beauty.

Olave came bustling out to meet them, disguising the undoubted triumph she had enjoyed since receiving Clara's letter. Undoubtedly, by now, the heiress would have found out for herself how stupid and unrewarding Charley was, and would prefer Ivor as soon as she set eyes on him again. He had grown increasingly handsome; too much so, his mother reflected grimly; it was time he settled down with a wife instead of seducing the housemaids. She would do her utmost, especially after dear Clara had departed, to throw the two young people together. 'I don't like picture-book girls,' Ivor had said fastidiously; certainly the departed parlourmaid had been plain. She, Olave, had pointed out reasonably that besides being very pretty, Sophy would be extremely rich. Ivor had shrugged and raised one of his peaked eyebrows, but at least was aware of the situation.

She said kindly now to the young woman, alighting from the carriage. 'You must refresh yourself, and then go down to see the bishop. He is in his study, and expects you. My sister and I have a great deal to say to one another, as you will understand.' Having delivered this broadside, she instructed the servants to take down Sophy's baggage from the top of the carriage: what an alarming number of hat-boxes! It was well seen the young person was spoilt.

Sophy was taken upstairs to her room, washed, let the maid comb out and dress her hair, flattened a trifle from the journey; and, once again herself, was escorted down to see the bishop.

Horace Pallant was in despair. He had hardly heard Olave's statement that young Miss Sophy would visit him this afternoon for the first of many instructive talks. He was as usual far more concerned with the state of his son's soul. In many ways, Ivor seemed to have no soul at all, and less heart; he jeered at good, and deliberately cultivated evil. The sons of clergy were said to be notorious in such ways, for some reason only known to the higher powers.

Horace Pallant had persevered in his intention to educate his son himself, but it was like looking into a sewer. Only yesterday, an attempt to placate Ivor by permitting him to translate from the Latin any passage he chose had resulted in a rendering, in flawless iambics, of some of the filthiest verses of Catullus. 'I'm too old to learn, father,' the boy had replied most impudently when reproved. It seemed, though he was clever, impossible to instil into him a love of quiet scholarship for its own sake; the only enthusiasm to be aroused in him was evidently to play fiercely on the cathedral organ, not always suitable music at that; and, of course, there was the late matter of the parlourmaid. That had grieved the bishop deeply, and not only because Olave said tall ones were difficult to get and if it had been one more of the housemaids, it would have mattered less. It was the principle of the thing, or rather the lack of any. The girl, of course, had had to go, although he himself had charitably written her some sort of character.

There seemed nothing more he could do except to sit now as he was doing, with his white head in his hands. He had aged twenty years in the past few months. Evil, he knew, should be driven out by prayer, but even prayer eluded him. All he could do was to think of the young man he had himself once been, full of generosity and hope, the youth of the Grand Tour, of Tuscany. Images long buried in his mind might save him, as God could not.

At this point Aphrodite herself, ripe and glorious as once glimpsed at Volturna, entered, wearing a green velvet gown and smiling with curved lips that had smiled thus ever since the seventh century B.C.

64

He heard himself saying thickly, 'Let me see your breasts.' He did not remember groping his way to where she had already seated herself, still smiling. Nor could he recall which of them had opened the green bodice. He surveyed, no longer in stone but in flesh, the most perfect globes he had ever beheld, laid his head with a happy sigh against their perfumed warmth; and was still. This was heaven, the pearly gates; and he asked nothing more.

Sophy herself kept still for some time, wondering when the bishop would move. Then the door opened and Ivor, whom she'd met at Grandfather Aaron's funeral and didn't like, stood there, his mouth smiling narrowly, his brilliant disquieting glance taking in everything.

'I say, I'd fasten yourself up if I were you,' he remarked. 'I think my pater's dead.'

He added that he would go and tell them, and left, closing the door. Sophy rose, carefully laying the bishop aside, and fastened up her bodice. She was sorry about the old gentleman, but she hadn't done any harm; he had looked sad when she came in, and had died cheerful; he was smiling now. Sophy thought of another thing which cheered her also; if the bishop really was dead, there would have to be another funeral. Perhaps Lord Tenterdowne would come back from Ireland for it.

7

THE bishop's funeral promised to be such a well-attended affair – the Archbishop himself had agreed to be present and to conduct the obsequies – that Olave admitted to herself that she was, reprehensibly, enjoying what was probably the last of her social importance as bishop's widow. Soon she would have to give way to some other woman, and the future held very little of interest. Now, there were the Arrangements. It followed that she could neither mourn, as would have been becoming – one might make an effort later on when the cathedral was full – or to attend to her young guest, Sophy. It suited her plans well enough, therefore, to leave Sophy in the hands of Ivor, come what might.

'Show her the cathedral, and in particular the organ, though of course you must not play it,' she told her son. He was in fact extraordinarily gifted as regarded music, she thought, and could play any instrument. It was a pity he could not, at present, show off in this way to Sophy; but the proximity of so handsome a young escort should arouse the girl's interest to a degree which might pay later dividends. More than that Olave did not admit to herself, knowing as she did that Ivor was not to be trusted alone with any female under forty-five at earliest. Within the depths of

Olave's awareness was the possibility that, were Ivor to compro-
mise Sophy as he had done the parlourmaid, it would be one way
of forcing the marriage and cause the money to become safely
theirs. Clara, when the matter was vaguely touched on, seemed
not to object to anything except the prospect of having the
young person back at Lawley. She appeared to have become most
unworldly. Shares – Olave, unlike most wives, had always had
access to her late husband's newspapers – in the Masterson
pottery were going up, in the mysterious way shares at times do.
Olave also kept in touch with two of her half-brothers, Ezra and
Amos, who managed certain commercial aspects of the pottery
rather than its aesthetic side: that was left to Nehemiah and
Jacob. Clara, less well informed than Olave of what ought to
interest her, showed no concern one way or the other. Her
thoughts were with the absent Tenterdowne, and it had occurred
to her that with Sophy out of the way by the time be returned, she
herself might perhaps be allowed to return to indexing for him
again.

Meantime, she kept fretting over the posts, waiting for word to
come that he had at least landed in Ireland safely.

Sophy was ushered by Ivor into the cathedral by its side door to
survey the bishop's coffin where it lay draped in purple, with his
mitre and crozier on top. Sophy stared in recognition at the
crozier: they had used, the *leucomones*, the priest-kings, to carry
them in Etruria, What had made her remember that? It was long,
long ago, in another life, it seldom came back to mind. It must
be the near presence of Ivor, who in some way had been present
also; but it wasn't the kind of thing she wanted to discuss.

She made herself come back to the present, and admire,
though she thought the whole thing was a pity, the pillars and

niches where, before the Reformation, saints' statues had stood. 'The organ was put in after all of that,' remarked Ivor, 'before it became sinful to think of music at services. There was a long time when it wasn't played, then I started to play it.'

She remained polite, but uninterested; his assurance made her remember how pleased he was with himself and how greatly she disliked him. There was no doubt that he was extremely handsome, and even less doubt that he knew it.

'It would be improper to play with the coffin present,' he observed, as if she had asked him to. 'If you will come with me I will show you the organ loft, however, and the pipes.'

She went, innocently. They mounted a circular staircase to a little wooden door, and inside, placed within a jutting carved balcony, was the great instrument itself, grey pipes rearing delicately and variously. Ivor struck one with his hand as if he could not bear that there should be no sound; a deep obedient echo came.

Sophy stared at the organist's seat, with a mirror above it so that the player could see the congregation and, no doubt, be told when to stop. She herself was not particularly fond of music. She looked at the reflection of the coffin far below, and the mitre and crozier. Etruria, long ages ago. It had receded; she was still here, in the cathedral. She turned to go down again, only to find that Ivor had closed and bolted the wooden door and was standing in the way, so that she could not push past him. He stood with arms folded, eyes narrowed to gleaming slits.

'And now, you little bitch, if I am not to tell Mama how I found you and my father, and what killed him, you will do as I say. She'll have the skin off your backside if you don't.'

The money, he had already agreed with Olave, would be useful.

*

Sophy hadn't wanted to be beaten again. That was why she'd agreed to it. The space between the organ-pedals and the seat was so small that she couldn't have got away from him anyway after he thrust her down. What followed was swift and cruel, not a bit like it had been with Lord Tenterdowne. Even her stepfather's belt had frightened and hurt her less. She could see Ivor's narrow face and red hair above her, jerking; it made the balcony seem to do the same thing, and the reflected bishop's coffin and mitre and crozier. She tried again to think of who she'd been, and who *he* had, and how they'd always disliked each other in past ages and never got on; and yet he was saying now, while he thrust deep into her, that she'd have to marry him or her reputation would be in shreds.

'You've been at it already, little bitch. Was it Tenterdowne? It can't have been Charley. He hasn't got the facilities.'

She began to cry, and said again that she was very fond of Charley. Ivor began to jeer.

'It's too late. I expect I'm giving you a baby, on purpose. You'll swell up like a pear, then you'll pup. You'll spurt milk till there's none left. Charley won't want you, nobody'll want you, and I don't myself, it's the money. Old Aaron made plenty of it, and I'll spend it, and if you don't do as you're bid for the rest of your life, I'll spread the story about the bishop all round town.'

It came to her that if Tenterdowne heard the story about the bishop, he mightn't know all the poor old man had done was to lay his head against her, then die. He might think she'd misbehaved, as was happening now with Ivor. She hadn't wanted it, didn't like Ivor; he was cruel. She didn't want his baby.

He left her at last, fastening himself. 'That's all for the time.

Charley wouldn't have anything like I've just shown you. I've seen him without his clothes in holidays, learning to swim. He didn't learn, he only floated because he's so fat. He isn't good at anything. Tie up your drawers, I've finished; were you expecting more?'

He laughed, turning away to unlock the door; and she was left with a strange feeling. Although she loathed Ivor, in a way she liked what he did. That was truly dreadful. She mustn't permit it again.

On the way out he turned to her, and she had a clear image of him which remained when they were apart: peaked chin in the pale narrow face, bright and terrible eyes set at a slight angle; pointed ears like a faun's or a devil's; a devil's. His slim body and long hands had pinched, squeezed, battered, bruised. He must have known he was making her like it, after all. She heard him speak now.

'Girls are all the same. They take to it in the end after squealing at the beginning.'

'I didn't squeal.' Tears were still running down her face; two black-clad women walking past looked at her with sympathy. It was touching to see how many young people mourned the dead bishop.

Despite Olave's efforts to promote their acquaintance, Sophy saw to it that she was not left alone with Ivor again. When his mother suggested, in the presence of company, that the two young people might care to talk a walk together in the garden, Sophy noted the surrounding bushes and firmly refused to be guided away from the middle of the lawn. Likewise, when they were directed to a window-seat together, she sat in full view.

However it was impossible to prevent Ivor's whisperings in her ear. He kept saying that she must give him a son because of Grandfather Aaron's will, which would never do her any good otherwise. 'Let me into your bedroom tonight.' She made sure of bolting the door.

He turned sulky after that. 'It's no pleasure to me, I assure you. I don't even like you. If it wasn't for the money you wouldn't see me for dust.'

'I loathe you,' she said often, under her breath. In fact she had begun to tremble at the sight of him, growing weak at the knees. She was convinced his mother knew what had happened, and wanted it to happen again. One thing Ivor said once however disgusted her, as it spoiled the memory of Tenterdowne's last words.

'You aren't made of sea-foam, you know. You were made out of what I put up you in the organ-loft, doing my best to make a baby. *That* belonged to a dirty old man like my grandfather, a god named Uranus. He wouldn't leave his wife alone and she was tired of giving birth, like you'll do in the end, you little bitch, whether you like it or not. Ge, that was her name, got their son Kronos to take his scythe and slice off the old god's balls as he flew back home over the Mediterranean, ready to make more children. He fled to the furthest star, and his balls fell down and spilled out their last foam into the sea, and that's where you come from, little bitch, and don't let anyone tell you otherwise. You ought to start feeling sick soon, ha, ha. I'm certain I managed it.'

It was at that point that she decided to marry Charley. It didn't matter what he had or what he hadn't. She would go with Lady Tenterdowne back to Lawley after the funeral, and be married to Charley as soon as it could be arranged. Then, if there was a baby, everyone would think it was his. The more she thought of the idea the better it seemed. She didn't like Charley's mother much, but she liked Mrs Pallant even less. It would be pleasant to deprive her and Ivor of the money.

All that was before the news reached them about John Tenterdowne.

8

HE, meantime, had driven across Wales without seeing it, unable to recall anything but the unbidden delight experienced when Sophy had come to his bed. That the situation should not recur was of course desirable. It was as well that he was on the way meantime to another country, with the sea between himself and temptation. He would stay in Ireland until he was cured of his illicit passion. Every mile ought to be making him forget.

Altogether he was in no state to withstand a rough tide from Fishguard, but dared not wait for a smoother crossing; he might return, in a new surge of weakness. He no longer recognised himself, and as all men and some women are aware, the tides running from Fishguard to Ireland are worse by far than those coming back the other way. Tenterdowne stopped at a Rosslare inn at last and drank down a large quantity of restorative brandy to calm his stomach and his mind. He was not given to drinking spirits, or to any form of intemperance; all he told himself was that he must now take in plenty of fresh air.

There were carriages for hire, and Tenterdowne approached one driver and said he himself must hold the reins. 'You may seat yourself inside and be a lord for the evening,' he remarked. It was by then getting almost dark, and they had a twenty-mile journey to make to the westward, then north. The driver shrugged, got in and seated himself, handing the long whip to the lord this evidently was, at least he'd said so and looked it, a very handsome gentleman, dressed like they were. They set off shakily, the road proved full of potholes, and grew worse the further they travelled.

Green Ireland was no more seen by John Tenterdowne than green Wales. He slashed in fury at the horses, filled with an anger partly induced by brandy and part by circumstances, the last a sudden crying need for Sophy. It was in this frame of mind that the equipage encountered that of Mad Johnny O'Toole, perched atop his ramshackle post-coach and driving hell for leather, as he did each night after the mails were done with, back to the inn to get drunk yet again. He was not drunk when the other carriage hit him, and sober enough to see for himself what happened next; the driver, a gent by the looks of him, toppled off the box, while the horses went screaming over as well, their reins dragging; there was a sound of splintering wood, and the other carriage lay helpless upside down on the road, its wheels whirling clear in air. Flung clear also, but lying still, with his neck broken, was the late gent who had driven.

The real owner clambered somehow out of the inside, where he had been trapped. He was cursing roundly as only an Irishman can.

'You'll pay for this, Johnny O'Toole, and you drunk as always. Himself is dead by the looks of him, and there's my car and hosses; they'll not run again in a while if ever. You'll pay, sor, you'll pay. It's taking you to court I'll be after this.'

'Take yourself there, for it was yours hit mine,' retorted the other, staring down at what had been an English lord. 'It's a pity of him, but maybe the best way to go,' he remarked. 'If you were knowing who he was, we could maybe tell them at the inn.'

9

THE bishop's funeral had been delayed to allow for a full convocation of clergy. In the end it proceeded, with the Archbishop in full lawn sleeves, lesser prelates following, vicars and clergy and the men of the congregation and the diocese. The late Horace Pallant had been well respected and everybody found the occasion moving.

The women had sat upstairs in the gallery, as by custom, the widow in black weepers which hid her face and concealed the fact that she looked less disturbed than anyone else present. The deep bell tolled and everyone rose to their feet as the coffin was carried out at last. Among them was Sophy, blind with tears, in her hand a black-edged letter. No doubt everyone thought she was crying for the bishop. Even the horrible organ-loft was blurred today, as well as thankfully silent.

A servant had brought the letter from Lawley, from the earl. It had been meant for Clara, but the servant had seen Sophy crossing from the house, had said he didn't like to disturb her ladyship till the service was over, and would Miss Sophy see that she got the letter with the sad news? 'It's a terrible thing that he's dead like that in Ireland, his poor lordship. The earl says it ain't

76

worth bringing the remains over, won't bring 'em back to life. They'll bury him there.'

That was how she'd heard that he was dead, the man she loved. She would never love anyone like that again. All round her were women who thought she was mourning for the bishop, whom she hadn't really known, and that it was right and proper. She, Sophy, knew none of her feelings were, had been, or ever would be right or proper. They were wrong and improper, as she knew very well, and by now didn't care.

She saw Ivor pass below holding his share of the pall, and looked away. After they all returned to the house she gave the earl's letter to Clara. 'It's bad news, I'm afraid,' she said. She didn't watch while Clara read the letter, but presently heard her gasp, then faint. She was borne out to lie down. Ivor came in, among the company, dressed like everyone else in black. He spoke into Sophy's ear, mockingly.

'Your nose is red with crying; blow it. Everyone will begin to think you were rather much too fond of my pater. Perhaps I ought to tell them you slept with Tenterdowne. I hear he's dead as well. Your tits are swelling, did you know? It happens quite soon in pod. Next thing, you won't be able to fasten your dresses.'

He sounded complacent, no doubt thinking she would have to decide to marry him. A wild hope had come to her that if she was with child, it might be Tenterdowne's. She would live with that hope while, as Ivor had put it, she swelled up like a pear. It wouldn't be possible to tell one way or the other until after that.

Later Olave came to her and said her sister was prostrated, but insisted on returning to Lawley tomorrow. 'I will go with her,' said Sophy firmly. 'I am going to marry Charley as soon as it can be arranged.'

Olave controlled her expression; the weepers helped. To have known Ivor – the precise degree of knowledge was still veiled from his mother – and still to want to marry that clout with mumps! It was the title, undoubtedly.

10

CHARLEY and Sophy were married at the earliest possible date, Charley's sixteenth birthday. She was in fact a little older, but was able to tell him that she'd waited for him, which cheered him immensely. He was easily pleased by a kind word or look; it wouldn't be unpleasant to have married him.

The ceremony took place privately in the drawing-room at Lawley, with no guests but, as witnesses, Clara and the earl. They were still in mourning, but instead of black Sophy had chosen a lilac dress, which was correct half-mourning; and carried a bunch of primroses. She'd picked those because John Tenterdowne was making them now, in Ireland. She often thought of him.

In the afternoon they went for a walk in the grounds, though not as far as the waterfall. In the evening they played chess, at which game Charley's slowness didn't matter. Then it was time to go to bed. Once there, Charley looked at his bride. How beautiful she was!

'I love you so much,' he said shyly. 'I – I don't want to hurt you.'

He was, truth to tell, in slight trepidation. He hadn't done anything of the kind before. The earl had instructed him, but Charley wasn't sure if he could manage it. His grandfather had, as usual, been talking in the language of the farm, and it seemed coarse to think of Sophy on the same level as Belinda, the earl's favourite Middle White.

Sophy assured him he wouldn't hurt her, which was true; nothing now could. She had ceased to have feeling and had never had morals. One lived for the moment; which proved to be, for the time, Charley's unwieldy body turned upon hers, puffing and panting. She aided him as best she could. He didn't achieve anything like Ivor, but that wasn't to be expected; for one thing Ivor was older. For another, she loathed Ivor and was fond of Charley. Perhaps he'd get better at it.

The weeks passed, and it became evident that Grandfather Aaron's money would soon be available. Sophy remained vague about dates, and such was Clara's relief that she didn't enquire too closely; after all, any child now born was legally Charley's. Nevertheless that time after mumps, the doctor had said – well, never mind. The earl was pleased. He remarked that now poor John was dead, he'd teach Charley to deal with the rents on Fridays now he'd proved himself. 'Tell him to come to the smaller drawin' room,' he added. 'I can't get up to the library these days. I'll stay with him while the tenants come, to show him what to do and how to do it. He seems willin' to learn.'

Friday came, and Charley obediently presented himself at the place arranged, seating himself beside his grandfather's bath-chair at a table on which the rent-books lay, their pages in neat columns. His father had been good at things of the kind; he wasn't. He tried to make sense and arithmetic of what happened when one tenant after another came in, pulled his forelock and advanced certain coins to the earl, who put them in a leather bag. By the end it was quite heavy.

80

'Now do the addin' up,' said the earl. 'We ought to have nineteen pounds, four shillings and eightpence. Have we?'

Charley didn't know, and miserably said so. 'Can't have the rents goin' wrong now you're inheritin' money,' said the earl gruffly. 'Don't think you only need do one thing well; pigs can do four or five.'

Charley said he would try. He was most anxious to please everybody, but always seemed to end by pleasing nobody; except that Sophy was always kind to him.

11

THE earl had raised his coffee-cup in salute to Sophy when her condition caused her briefly to leave the breakfast-table. Otherwise matters modified themselves somewhat through the management of Clara, who was naturally anxious that things should proceed unhindered. Her first action was to ensure that Charley and Sophy no longer slept together; she arranged separate rooms. It was safer, she said. Charley was sad, but Sophy was reasonable; she remembered how Cécile Volanges had had a miscarriage behind the bedroom door as a result of too much carrying-on with her seducer. It was not that poor Charley could be described in any such way; it was more like parting company with a large and affectionate dog.

However she was as anxious as everybody else for Grandfather Aaron's money to be released. Not too much remained by now at Lawley, large sums having been spent on the late John Tenterdowne's library, with which of course Clara would never part. Otherwise, Clara's advice seemed sound, and the months passed peacefully. The earl had made a mild profit over the price of bacon.

Sophy was however growing bored. It wasn't only that, as horrible Ivor had predicted, her dresses wouldn't fasten easily these days; in addition, there was nothing much to do, as Clara kept full charge of the household and Sophy could not honestly say that she minded; her heart had never been given to domestic matters. Nevertheless it was sad to go to the library to read now no incomparable grey head could be seen at the desk; in any case she'd only liked poetry and French. Chess with Charley passed the afternoons, especially if it rained. On Fridays she had begun to try to help him with the rents, but had to give that up; she wasn't any better at accounts than he was, and things were getting into a muddle even before she grew too large to show herself with, as Clara put it, propriety before the tenants. *You'll swell up like a pear, then you'll pup. You'll spurt milk till there's none left.* Long ago, a goddess, not herself, had spurted milk out into the heavens, and it was called the Milky Way, a galaxy of stars. She didn't feel inclined for that sort of thing, it was too public.

She would in any case be glad when it was all over, even if it meant sleeping with Charley again. He still gazed at her with adoration in his blue-grey eyes, no matter what shape she had become.

Ivor and his mother called at Lawley in the seventh month, and Sophy felt uncomfortable under the gaze of both, one sardonic and the other hostile. Olave said proudly that Ivor was about to go to the new kingdom of the Hellenes as an attaché in the Diplomatic Service. A friend of the late bishop's had arranged it. Well, that would at least take Ivor out of the way for some time, till after the birth. Meanwhile, she didn't feel like sewing things for the baby, as was evidently expected of her; she hated sewing.

To Clara's annoyance and Sophy's unease, Olave Pallant drove over again to be present at the actual birth, making out that she must support Clara in any eventuality. The thought of being an eventuality did not appeal to Sophy in the least, and she objected to Olave's prying and to her solid, constant presence by the bed, armed with knitting. Clara sat on the other side with no employment; the sad, unfinished Berlin woolwork slippers for John Tenterdowne had been left upstairs. She was the better able to keep an eagle eye.

The labour started, Sophy bit her lips, and Charley was brought in to kiss his wife and wish her well. 'Remember I love you,' he whispered, and the withdrawal of his great doting moon of a face was, most ungratefully, a relief. She didn't feel like seeing any men at all at present, or ever.

The pains continued, and were sharp; she had never imagined it would be as bad as this. The presence of the two women made her unwilling to cry out. Nevertheless the sweat broke out on her forehead, and when Olave leant over to wipe it with a cloth wrung out in cold water Sophy found herself screaming 'Go away. Go away. Go away.'

'She's feverish,' said Olave, and sat down again. There was nobody but the two sisters in attendance; Clara had told the servants they would not be required. She and her sister knew what to do. They looked, in fact, like two spectators watching a contest, each with sizeable stakes in whoever won. Sophy writhed and groaned with pain. She had hardly thought of her mother Hannah all these years, but wished she were here now instead of these two eager-eyed women, each intent on one thing only; money, a great deal of money. If she herself should die – and the pain began to make her think she might – or if it was a girl, everything would have to be done again or else be distributed between Matthew and Mark and Luke and Johnny at the kilns, and Samuel and Joseph and Elijah and Ezekiel and young Amos, who had been the butler at one point, aged fifty-two. Aaron had employed the Old and New Testament extensively at the births of his sons by various mothers, evidently thinking that it would give them a veneer of respectability otherwise denied them. At any rate, Sophy thought between intervals of bearing down, if they were rich they would soon be respectable; that was what the world was like. She herself felt thousands of years old.

She had hoped to delay things till Olave at last went off to bed, but the child wouldn't stay inside her much longer. Midnight came and passed, and Olave and Clara were still sitting there, like two birds of ill omen. Omen. Augury. There had been an eagle once that flew towards Rome, and Tanaquil had told her husband Tarquinius Priscus it was an augury, and to follow the eagle. Tarquin had done so and had become first king there; it was all nonsense about Romulus, she'd been watching from somewhere herself. Since then, the Emperor Napoleon . . . an eagle . . . .

Forget the pain; remember instead. Remember augurs; slain animals' livers which foretold the future; strange gods, a forgotten tongue. Flutes played at the burial of the dead, and myrtle crowns. She didn't want to die; that woman, brooding at the bed out of the underworld, aaahhh . . . .

The child was born. It was a boy, with red hair and eyes whose colour nobody would ever see, as it was dead, strangled by the cord. Its mouth, opened early in a desperate attempt to find air, still bore the archaic, triangular smile of the Apollo of Veii.

'You wicked, ungrateful girl,' screamed Clara, thrusting the child's congested face in front of Sophy's tear-filled eyes.

'All to do again,' remarked Olave smoothly, her eyes bland with triumph.

Clara laid the dead baby aside and blew her nose. She was in too much distress to realise that she shouldn't have let Olave see it. The latter gave a little tight smile like her son's and rose, leaving the birth-chamber.

Presently, attending to the afterbirth, they heard her carriage drive away. Her expression was still placid, in fact anticipatory. She'd thought as much. Ivor didn't seem to be paying much attention to his duties in Athens, judging from all one heard. Charley's mumps had evidently weighted matters in Ivor's favour; shortly, he must return.

Out of motherly solicitude, Clara did not show Charley the baby, and he never knew that it had been anyone's but his. He came to see Sophy, visit and comfort her. He was almost the only person concerned who failed to say it would all have to be done again. Having cried with exhaustion and disappointment of a general kind, Sophy slept. At least the bishop's widow had gone away.

After Sophy had recovered her strength, Clara put her straight back into Charley's bed, and Charley himself was given, nightly, nourishing broth containing a good dose of pennyroyal. Clara was adamant that the former disgraceful business should not recur, especially as Olave wrote to say Ivor might be home by the year's end; he didn't seem suited to diplomacy, though he felt at home in Greece. Clara determined that before Ivor showed his face at Lawley, a baby of Charley's and no other should be on the way, without doubt or hesitation.

The young pair were meantime subject to a strict régime, pennyroyal broth apart; questions asked once a month, all walks supervised and accompanied by Clara in person, no riding because it might disturb things once they'd started.

Charley did his best to oblige, as always. His mother had him examined by the doctor again; the latter said his performance would improve with confidence. However Sophy still did not conceive, though a second medical examination revealed nothing wrong with her. It all went on for so long, and they were both so weary of the situation and the increasing lack of money, that it was almost a relief to hear that Ivor had come home, supposedly on furlough. However all who knew anything were aware that he'd made himself thoroughly undiplomatic at the embassy, and had been sent home.

12

IT had been glorious summer weather, and Olave had written to suggest that as she had certain things to discuss in private with dear Clara, would it be suitable if she were to be driven down on Friday afternoon? Perhaps Sophy could be sent for a walk.

Fiendish ingenuity had not, as it happened, been employed in the arrangement, as Olave was unaware of Friday afternoons as especially significant, being the day when Charley laboured, with heavy breaths and weaving tongue, over the estate accounts, which were becoming increasingly tangled. She had merely been prompted by a magnanimous fate.

Clara reflected sourly, on reading the letter, that no time had been given to her to reply as to suitability or otherwise. In plain words, she had no choice. She was feeling sullen in any case; strictures and pennyroyal simply hadn't worked, and Aaron Masterson still had no legitimate grandson.

On the afternoon in question, as Olave's carriage wheels sounded in the drive, Clara told Sophy she might go out in the park alone for an hour. 'No riding, mind; only a little walk, for gentle exercise.'

She sounds as if I'm a horse myself, thought Sophy resentfully.

She replied somewhat pertly that Elizabeth of Bohemia had had eleven children who all grew up, and used to ride every day while expecting.

'Well, her mother was Danish,' replied Clara unaccountably.

Olave swept in, and without delay seated herself on the sofa and began what she had come to say.

'It's two years now, Clara. Something will have to be done. That attack of mumps has quite clearly put Charley out of the running.'

It was Clara's turn to resent equine language, and she flushed a little, it was time Charley's mumps were consigned to oblivion in the collective memory.

'That being the case,' continued Clara, I have a suggestion regarding what dear Papa would perhaps have described as partnership, the shares, in the event, being equally divided. It has already been proved, as you know, that Ivor was not affected by mumps, which he got over when young. Had Sophy's choice been otherwise—'

Had it been otherwise, you and Ivor wouldn't have done a thing for us, Clara thought furiously; but she put as good a face on it as might be done. At the same time, she mentioned the probable matter of red hair; if that should again occur, would the proportion of payment perhaps be a little less? There was a certain risk of recognition involved.

'That would not signify, as any child born within Sophy's marriage is legally her husband's, and colour was not specified one way or the other in Papa's will,' Olave replied firmly.

There was only one thing the two good ladies failed to work out in the end or even consider, whether or not Sophy herself agreed to such an arrangement. They even settled it for recurrent Friday afternoons, in the spare bed upstairs, safe and private behind drawn curtains.

Sophy was enjoying her walk, and had gone quite a long way; it was after all nobody's business if she wasn't back within the hour. She wanted, once more, to visit the waterfall, sit there alone for a little while and think of John Tenterdowne. By now, he glimmered in her memory like a ghost. She wanted peace to remember him, and there hadn't been much lately.

It was odd to think – she stared between the summer trees – that she herself was Lady Tenterdowne now. It might have meant something very different. Sophy stared next at the windflowers, beginning this month to open in a greyish drift beneath the trees. They had purple stains against a golden heart, among the pale petals. There was a legend about Adonis turning into a windflower, the stain signifying his heart's blood. For some reason, the remembrance hurt Sophy. Perhaps John Tenterdowne was making windflowers now in Ireland as well as primroses last month. He was making the earth blossom, and would each year.

Sophy bent and picked a flower, gazing into its heart; then looked up, aware of a second presence. Ivor Pallant. She didn't ask what he was doing here or why he had come, or how he knew she would be in the home wood today. She only realised that in the whole course of marriage with Charley she hadn't once felt the strange sensation Ivor could arouse in her at sight and knew it. It was happening now, and he was advancing.

'Tired of marriage yet?'

His jeering laughter came; her knees were weak already. He didn't speak, only strode over and took her by the waist with two hands, tossing her down lightly among the windflowers.

'You will think of nobody but me,' he said.

She knew that, afterwards, she would find herself alone, crushed and bruised like the delicate, lumescent carpet on which she lay. She would have to explain the bruises to Charley somehow. He'd be disturbed at sight of them.

Ivor Pallant shortly began to feel his cool, ready seed run and flow copiously in this fool of a young woman, who didn't seem to like it, a fact which interested him not at all; he was merely obeying orders. While he lay within her, he let his mind stray backwards towards Greece, which he had lately left and where he had felt unusually at home. He'd visited the island where his mother Latona long ago had given him birth, and had stared at its proud ancient stone lions. Poseidon, helpful for once, had caused the island to rise out of the sea to spite Hera, Zeus' sister-wife, who was jealous of Latona, beloved by Zeus. (That meant his grandfather was his father.) The whole thing was too much, and after recalling Delphi and his other shrines Ivor returned idly to contemplation of what other men would always find irresistible, but he'd never liked Sophy, she wasn't flat-chested enough. She was writhing, no doubt with pleasure. He nipped her thigh, for no reason except principle.

'I'm making you like it, same as last time. Perhaps there'll be a baby again. You'll swell up again, then start to howl and have it.' He was glad to be a man, after all, He saw her head turn aside so that her cheek lay against the crushed windflowers.

'I loathe you. I've said it before. Don't ever touch me again.'

'I shall touch you as often as I please. My mater's arranging matters now with Charley's. The money must be made available. Even a fool like you can understand that, no doubt. I've finished, for the time, but I'll come back. Aunt Clara will tell you what to do.'

91

She won't, thought Sophy, and rebellion rose. Nobody considered anything but money. She might have had no feelings. That was the Mastersons, if you liked; if you don't succeed at first, keep trying. That was how Grandfather Aaron had grown rich. At present, Sophy rather wished he hadn't. She didn't watch Ivor go off, but lay on for a time, cheek turned against the ruined flowers on the ground, beneath the trees' shadow.

Presently she rose, and, moving with surprising steadiness, walked back to the house and into the kitchen, asking for a jug of vinegar. Then she went upstairs to where it was private, as the old women were still talking; and douched herself. She'd forgotten who told her that always worked. She wanted the money as much as anyone, and understood that she must have a son; but he wasn't going to be Ivor Pallant's. Almost anybody else would do.

'It only needs persuasion,' said Olave. Her eyes brooded. Clara sipped her tea. Since the death of John Tenterdowne her nature had hardened till it was almost as ruthless as her half-sister's.

'Perhaps the offer of a London season as a reward later on,' she ventured. 'Sophy has had, after all, a very dull time for the past few years; the prospect of diversion—'

'That cannot be afforded till the money's certain. You were always inclined to put the cart before the horse. There can be a very handsome season indeed once Sophy delivers the goods, as dear Papa used to say; but until then, as she is still obstinate, there is only one thing to do. I have a supple rod, and presumably you have a bucket of brine somewhere in the cupboards, or can obtain some. The exercise in question may be necessary more than once, and if the rods dry out they are of less effect.'

Clara was horrified; she'd never beaten the servants. 'She says she loathes Ivor, and does not want to set eyes on him again,' she replied desperately; she still disliked the thought of violence in any circumstances, particularly within the family.

'She need not; his part can be done in the dark if preferred,' said Olave in her practical way. 'He can arrive after midnight. It is only a short step for her along the corridor from where she sleeps with Charley.'

'I fear she will not agree,' said Clara, who knew more of Sophy's stubbornness than her sister. Olave merely smiled grimly, and said she'd bring the rod.

'I won't,' reiterated Sophy. 'I've had enough of the whole business. I intend to remain a devoted wife to Charley.' She had in fact done her best in such ways, as had he.

Clara put in sourly that there would be no roof left over her head, let alone Charley's, unless the books were balanced by money coming in; Charley still had no notion of accounting, and his grandfather, who helped at times, couldn't live for ever.

'Leave it to me,' said Olave when she heard. 'We must compel her. It will take two of us to hold the young woman down.'

Sophy was screaming. The pain and indignity of being birched like a servant, with old Clara holding up her nightdress with one hand and keeping the other on her back to hold her down against the bed's end, while Olave wielded the brine-supple rod, was unspeakable. It was worse than labour pains, because they at least produced something or other. Now, unless she agreed to go to bed with Ivor every Friday afternoon till she conceived, she'd be whacked like this every night; they'd said so. Ow. Ow, It was worse by far than her stepfather's belt, It was worse than – worse than – ow – worse perhaps than having to sleep with Ivor. After eight or nine of the best, Sophy agreed, tears streaming down her face.

'That is sensible,' said Olave, who appeared to control the situation. 'You will need a few days to recover; at present you will be unable to lie on your back. Let us say Friday, at three o'clock; and if you fail to appear—'

'I won't fail,' said Sophy sullenly. Clara was pulling down her nightgown again over the weals. They had risen bright red all over her buttocks, the latter's peach-bloom perfection marred. This sight later on greatly distressed Charley, who at once offered to pick out the bits of bark. He kissed the places; he was really very affectionate. The salt stung. 'I can't think what made my mother so unkind,' Charley said. 'You'll have to sleep on your face.'

He had a soul above money, and the implications of the whole business were entirely lost on him. Mama was talking of employing a bailiff for the arithmetic, and said he, Charley Tenterdowne, must sit and watch the man add. That would make him look foolish, he knew, in front of the tenants and his grandfather. Charley was aware that he was stupid; too stupid for Sophy, who was so beautiful and loving. He knew she wanted him to give her a baby, but he couldn't even try while she was sleeping on her face, having sobbed into the pillow for a long time. Poor Sophy. Perhaps she'd be better in a day or two, whatever had gone wrong meantime with Mama.

Clara, who as stated had developed an iron streak in her nature since the death of Tenterdowne, had decided finally to hurt Charley's feelings and employ the bailiff. The earl couldn't be expected to correct and supervise accounts at his age any longer. They couldn't afford an extra salary either, but it would have to be done and might pay off in the end. She had advertised and, herself, interviewed several applicants. The one selected in the end was eccentric, but cheap. From his references Mr Laverty seemed efficient, though his appearance was hardly that of a gentleman. Asked if he would find it solitary here in the stable-quarters (they only kept one carriage-pony now) he replied that he preferred solitude. He liked to practise his oboe in his spare time, and it was preferable to be away from neighbours.

That had been some days ago now, and the accounts, with Charley still sitting watching how it ought to be done, seemed already to have improved. The episode with the rod had however had to be repeated, though Sophy was by now mostly submissive. Last week, Olave had arranged things successfully; the week before that Sophy had concealed herself in the attics till it was too late; as Ivor had furiously remarked, they might have saved him the trouble of coming down; that great idiot Charley would walk in any minute, having finished messing up his columns. Sophy had burst into yet more tears, saying Charley wasn't an idiot, and Ivor was loathsome.

It could not be denied that of the two sisters, dear Olave was the more efficient; and today she, Clara, was nervously taking her turn again as supervisor and hoping everything would go off this time as planned. She herself had lately rescued the Berlin wool-work slippers intended earlier for dear John, and was finishing them; they could after all go to some deserving cause. However it was impossible not to overhear the conversation beyond the bed-curtains.

'Now you've had your bottom whipped again, you ought to come on faster. I haven't got all day.'

'I loathe you. I'm getting tired of saying it.'

'Perhaps a further gentle touch from the willow, broom or

95

birch from my mater? She'd come over specially early next week.'

'Leave me alone. It wouldn't make any difference. The whole thing's a waste of time and effort.' Sophy sounded, Clara thought, almost smug.

'I'll show you whose time is being wasted, you little bitch. Don't spit, it's rude. Do as you're told. There, that's better; much, much better. Catherine the Great used to make her lovers bring her on by spanking her first. Otherwise she was getting past it.'

Ivor was bored. In fact, he had other fish to fry. He had fallen in love with a girl named Daphne, whom he'd met at a party given by her father at the Greek Embassy. Ivor wanted to marry her, but the old man wouldn't permit it until he showed signs of being able to support a wife. Daphne herself kept running away. If only Sophy would start her baby! It ought to have happened by now; he'd done his best. Mama and Aunt Clara always made Sophy undress, thinking no doubt that it would interest him. It didn't; the sight, which would have made other men end up drooling, seemed to Ivor like having to wallow in pink ice-cream. Daphne, on the other hand, was slim and boyish. They'd talked briefly about gardens. She would like, she said, a little house with a garden and a shrubbery, to hide in. She—

'I'm *not* past it. I simply loathe you. Ugh. Oh—'

'Ha, ha. I knew you'd come any minute. Women are all the same. Listen to yourself.'

The ecstasy began, despite everything. Clara found herself staring at the trembling curtains, listening to Sophy's moans of induced pleasure. Her own tears trickled down on to the forgotten Berlin woolwork. She and John had never got as far.

Perhaps, she decided, she'd loved him too much to dislike anything at all that happened, because so little had. If going down into the underworld like Ishtar would bring him back, she'd go; even if, like that goddess, she had to remove all her clothes on the way down, one by one, till she stood naked in front of the jealous queen of hell. It all sounded most improper, and one could not even remember clearly if, after all that trouble, Ishtar had retrieved her husband in the end or not. They hadn't been much heard of since.

A rustling sound came from the concealed bed, the curtains parted and Ivor came out, fastening himself. He closed one eye at his aunt, then went out, leaving the door open behind him. He had not, come to think of it, grown up into a mannerly person at all. Clara thrust the needle into the canvas, rose, and called out tactfully to Sophy, still unseen.

'Lie as you are for some minutes; it is beneficial.' Then she went out and closed the door after her. Sophy had already prepared to swing her legs off the bed and dive towards the commode, inside which the jug of vinegar reposed, covered by a circular white thread cloth in crochet, weighted round the edge with coloured beads. The vinegar had worked, so far. She'd give it a day or two to wear off, during which time she'd tell those two old women a baby had started, to fend off Ivor. Then, before the man's free day at the end of the week, she would visit the new bailiff for the first time to make sure his quarters were comfortable. Revenge was sweet, and nobody would know for nine months.

Charley, meantime, had been sitting beside the new bailiff to try to understand how things ought to be done. He was honestly anxious to learn, although the man was repulsively ugly and Charley, in his undemanding way, worshipped beauty before all else. However Clara had decided that a handsome, or even a presentable, bailiff might be dangerous as well as expensive. Mr Laverty seemed humble, having no great opinion of his own abilities although, as the afternoon wore on, he caught out four of the tenants who had done Charley out of change, and made them pay up. Charley flushed beetroot-red at the uncovering of his folly; and asked Mr Laverty if he was quite happy in the stable quarters, as a cottage from one of the dishonest tenants could be made available to provide him with neighbours. 'You'd find out what's going on,' ventured Charley, who hardly knew for himself. However Mr Laverty – one always paid a bailiff the respect of a handle – said he could see to hisself, had done it ever since the wife died, could manage, and didn't want no company.

His appearance was startling and he smelt, being one of those unfortunate persons who start to do so almost immediately after sluicing themselves down daily first thing at the yard pump. Charley realised he couldn't help it, or in fact anything regarding his general undoubted notability. He had a shock of black hair, which tapered down to a rather miserable goatee beneath his chin. His body was ungainly and ill-proportioned, and he walked, when he did so, with the rolling gait of a sailor on shore leave for the time being only. He swore when asked that he'd never been to sea, having formerly kept the books in several pubs. His features themselves were undistinguished, except for the straight line from his low animal forehead to the tip of his nose in profile, a trait which can mean that its owner is good at active sports.

Charley vainly tried to understand the books after Mr Laverty had copied everything out again for him in a fair round hand. The tenants, despite his open disgrace, had pulled their forelocks to him but not to the bailiff, it didn't seem right. Mr Laverty; was after all the one who'd done the arithmetic. A vague awareness of the inequality of social distinctions reached Charley's sluggish, amiable brain. He would turn the whole thing over in his mind later on, with Sophy. He might as well have been with her all afternoon.

He was sad that evening at dinner, because Mama said he mustn't continue to sleep with Sophy at present; there was to be a dear little baby. He was however permitted to give Sophy a good-night kiss, and she took him in her arms and said again how fond she was of him, and they'd see each other during the day. He went to bed alone, but happy; and Sophy examined what conscience she possessed. She knew, had known for some time although she hadn't let him guess it, that Ivor had made her like certain things very much, although she still loathed him personally. The oddity of the situation occurred to her, but it couldn't be helped; she wanted it increasingly, and what poor Charley could do was simply not enough. She wouldn't, of course, ever tell him so. That would be most unkind.

Early in the following week, Sophy managed to slip along to the stables when she was supposed to be lying down. She'd broken the news of a pregnancy to the two old women. 'You don't look like it,' Olave had remarked suspiciously. 'Are you certain? What are your dates?'

Sophy had replied that she could hardly be expected to give exact dates yet; once a week had been too often. Clara looked indulgent and said she'd arrange the separate room. Olave broke in again; she wasn't convinced.

'If this is a trick you're playing, my girl, you will be severely disciplined, and the whole thing will have to start again.'

Altogether she'd tried to be sick over her breakfast egg to reassure everybody, but hadn't managed more than a burping noise, having deliberately swallowed some air.

As she came closer to the stables, a mournful hooting sound came from the upstairs quarters. Sophy was curious to find out what it was in any case, and picked up her skirts, ascending past the scent of fresh hay. The pony was still out in the near field, grazing; it was thoughtful of Mr Laverty to have filled the rack. The pony took the earl back and forth to the home farm regularly, but not much else these days; there were few occasions, because there wasn't much money. Sophy told herself she was going to make some, then they'd see.

She scratched at the upstairs door and entered, although Mr Laverty was still playing his oboe. The first thing Sophy noticed was the smell. It was goatlike, but at least it was a he-goat. She rather liked goats anyway. The bailiff looked up at sight of her and didn't seem surprised, but merely asked if her ladyship would mind if he just finished the bit he was at? 'I only does it to remind me of the wife,' he said. 'Bought it when she died. It's not that I'm much good at it, but it reminds me of her, like.'

Sophy nodded, smiled and wondered if his wife had hooted. When he had finished what sounded like a dirge, she asked what his wife's name had been, to sound polite. He said it had been Syrie, after some French queen's song she'd written herself. Syrie's father, he vouchsafed, had been in the wars with Boney, but on our side. He'd just taken a fancy to the name, somehow. Sophy asked then if Syrie had been dead long; Mr Laverty still seemed inconsolable, but she'd try in a minute.

'Two years,' replied the widower, 'but a man can't keep to hisself always, not in some things. A slip of a thing, Syrie was. It was cholera finished her. That ain't pleasant to watch happen. Don't ever try.'

The sad dark stare of ancient Greece, with reeds swaying in a river, surveyed her. Mr Laverty laid down his oboe, and stood up. He was really a very odd shape; she hadn't noticed it before. The smell of goats increased.

Sophy didn't say more, and merely went to where a dilapidated horsehair sofa, with half its stuffing out, stood on three legs, the fourth being missing; opened her bodice, and lay down. Presently the sofa began to rattle. There had been no need for further words.

After a satisfactory interlude she made ready to go. Mr Laverty closed one eye, said 'Any time,' and held the door for her. As she descended the stairs she heard the oboe strike up again. She hoped the baby would have black hair, and wouldn't smell, but perhaps both aspects were too much to hope for.

Two things happened soon, or perhaps three, as Sophy found she was certainly pregnant. Firstly, one day Mr Laverty was no longer there, having absconded with his oboe and the money from the rents. The police were informed, but he was never traced. The other thing – and Sophy, who had a kind heart, felt sorry for him – was that Ivor was desolate, at least for the moment. Daphne had written to him to say she preferred to become a nun. He had become silent and morose, and was hardly even interested at the news of a coming baby, supposed to be his.

13

SOPHY had determined that this time, the two harpies should not be present on either side of her bed like avid gamblers each with a bet placed on the birth. Although she was by now extremely large and already feeling the child's weight drag at her, she merely arranged with two of the maids to have plenty of hot water ready and to lock the bedroom door. Also, she went to find the earl, who was playing billiards by himself from his bathchair, which made the game illegal as both feet are supposed to be on the floor.

'Please take Ivor, if he is brought, and Charley to see the pigs,' she said, 'and keep them there till everything is over.'

As she had foreseen, Olave came, and brought Ivor with her. Sophy did not subject herself to his by now morose gaze, but firmly locked herself in and heard the pony-trap drive off as arranged; there was no nonsense about the earl, he was reliable. She had already started the pains, and it shouldn't take long.

Presently Clara came and knocked on the door, demanding admittance. Sophy instructed the maids to refuse. 'I will reward you, never fear,' she told them, as they looked frightened. As she correctly guessed, the fear was less for old Lady T., who could be got over, than for that Mrs Pallant and all she stood for.

However they saw to the birth, being told by Sophy, who kept a clear head throughout, exactly what to do. The child was born without complications, and had black hair. It was large, alive, plump, and a girl. Sophy turned her head dismally to the wall. Perhaps Charley would suppose, again, that it was his.

She sent the baby, who on emerging had howled on a strange low note like an oboe, to be inspected by the two older women in the drawing-room. The maid who had been carrying it came back with it, saying her old ladyship had given a strange gurgling noise and fallen to the floor, and Mrs Pallant was attending to her and they'd sent for the doctor.

Rage, both at the child's sex and its obvious paternity, had induced a seizure in Clara; she never spoke again. Olave, as it chanced, had never set eyes on Mr Laverty. Sophy told the maids to bind her breasts up and send for the wet-nurse she'd arranged in any case. Feeding a baby spoiled one's figure, and last time there had been plenty of milk and nobody to drink it. She had determined, during the labour, that, money or no money, life could not be spent forever in this occupation.

Clara died shortly of a second seizure, and Sophy, by then recovering rapidly, knew she was her own mistress at last. She sent for Olave after the funeral, and that lady's murderous expression made it already clear that she was aware the fifty-fifty arrangement no longer pertained. However Sophy had certain alternatives.

'If you will take little Clara,' she said, 'I will pay you an allowance.'

'Where are you going to get the money?' Olave was suspicious as always.

'It will be arranged,' said Sophy. 'Your sister's namesake and your godchild is better with you than with me.'

Olave agreed unwillingly; a child would be a tie, but on the other hand she could try out various educational theories. The small Clara would be disciplined from the start, reared to think of herself as equally intelligent with men, and should end as a schoolmistress. Sophy had no illusions on that matter and less interest. She saw the dark head go off in the carriage in Olave's lap without any feelings at all except relief.

She had already dealt with Ivor, who had a brief flaring-up of what sounded like a recurrence of his former rages. 'If I'd been free of you and your Friday afternoons, and that brat isn't mine anyway, I could somehow have got Daphne in a corner, and they wouldn't have accepted her after that in the convent,' he said. 'The whole thing's your fault. I don't know what to do next. I don't want to sleep with you again, they'd ask questions at the pottery about red hair. Grandfather's sons were on the alert last time, you know, but they didn't see the result, which was fortunate.' He sounded almost animated.

'Console yourself,' Sophy said. 'We are going to let Lawley, failing the money from the will. We will move to London, where you will perhaps help me earn a living.' She smiled radiantly. An occasional escort, other than poor Charley, would be useful. So would a doorman.

Charley himself was still in tears at having to part with his fat little daughter, but Sophy persuaded him that the child would benefit greatly from sea air, as Olave had arranged to go to Scarborough to move in with her stepmother. Margaret, by now at a great age, still enjoyed the jointure old Aaron had left her, and was accordingly by far the most well-heeled of anybody. Also, she tended to feel giddy these days and would be glad of company, even Olave's. The child Clara would be welcome provided she was kept quiet.

They went off, and Sophy busied herself with finding tenants for Lawley and with renting, in expectation, a small convenient house just off Piccadilly.

The earl had not been forgotten. Grieved as he was at parting with his pigs, he would travel down once a month to make sure they flourished, and meantime there was a Bonapartist breeze blowing in London and he might no longer be ostracised. It was a better idea, he agreed, than waiting interminably for a live male birth for money they could make anyway. He assured Sophy she had all the attributes of a Middle White, and more.

'I'm not a sow,' said Sophy with reproach.

'Meant it as a compliment, m'dear. Pigs are intelligent as well as fertile. They have clean habits if left to themselves instead of bein' shut in a sty. You can graze a pig on grass and it'll turn it into a lawn, but nobody does because nobody ever has. It's like the late Emperor; there was nothin' like him seen since Julius Caesar, and both of 'em were assassinated because of plain envy.' He was convinced, like some, that Napoleon had been poisoned on St Helena; he hadn't died old, it was convenient, that was all.

He fell silent, and Sophy tried to cheer him by saying they'd take the billiard table with them to London and site it on the ground floor, where he could play all day, view incoming clients and even arrange matches, if that was the word; so many terms in billiards were different, mace, cue, spot, cannon and hazard all meaning something far other than the usual.

Besides letting the house, estate and shooting – the resident farmer was to stay – Sophy advertised in suitable gazettes read by bibliophiles. It was sad to think of parting with John Tenterdowne's library, but it was too immense to take, and if left to tenants would certainly be pilfered. She was gratified when, first before anyone, a tall, slender, deaf and no longer very young man came, was charming, examined a number of the volumes carefully and then made an offer for the whole. It was beyond anything she had dared to hope for. His clear, kindly eyes surveyed her with open admiration.

'I have never been able to hear very well, but at this present moment am very thankful that I can see,' he said. He didn't mean the books. Sophy blushed, then curtseyed. He had been announced simply as Devonshire.

He looked at a gold fob watch he wore, said he must be going, paid the whole, and arranged for the books to be conveyed to Chatsworth. Sophy saw *Les Liaisons* and the poetry go with grief, but it all added up, and the former volume had nothing to teach her by now. Also, she had made a useful acquaintance in the Duke of Devonshire, who might perhaps call on her in London; she'd given him the address.

II

The Best Society

1

THE removal had taken place without a single hitch, and Sophy greatly enjoyed furnishing the little new house, though the earl complained bitterly of the constant noise of horse-traffic along Piccadilly and, still more so, of an organ-grinder with a monkey who came and played daily beneath the windows. Sophy now and again gave money, as she liked the monkey, in its red coat, but hadn't much ear, she again admitted, for music.

'It's not music and never was,' growled the earl. Otherwise he was enjoying life, even at his age; he could play billiards all day, and a scoreboard had been set up for Sophy's pending clients, who could come and play for an extra fee in the intervals of French conversation. The last took place upstairs, where the earl could not go; he had his quarters behind the billiard-room. Ivor, on the other hand, inhabited the basement, which had once been a wine-cellar. Ivor had no recourse to the bottle, but drowned his sorrows in music, namely a Hungary zither he had acquired, and whose sad and plangent notes now and again came up to Sophy in the intervals of arranged instruction.

This had become a success, having been started off on the right foot by the Duke's card glimpsed in the hall. Sophy was sorry that Devonshire had not see fit to come in person, but possibly he knew French already. The card brought a number of distinguished acquaintances, and they sat on the circular couch, covered with crimson velvet, which Sophy had purchased and which was ideal for her purposes. Its shape allowed the conversations to take place either side by side, or else back to back, depending on the client. There were four concentric velvet-covered divisions, and a cherub on top.

A further gorgeous and useful acquisition was her bed. It had pale-blue drapes and stood in the further apartment, with the door open. Beyond that again was a large marble bath with brass taps, some emitting water and others sweet essences. It had been costly, but was the nearest thing to returning to sea-foam in London, and Sophy used it frequently.

She had inserted a further modest advertisement in the newspapers to the effect that ladies as well as gentlemen might be instructed in the niceties of spoken French, following an interview at the Piccadilly address. This was to ensure her respectability. Ladies who thereafter called were reassured by the sight of billiards and the earl, who was beginning to be accepted again in society; a title was a title, and there had been a great many changes in France. Charley chalked up the score when told what it was, and altogether Sophy at times felt free to take one of the new hackneys and have herself driven about London. It wasn't convenient to keep a carriage in town unless one had a mansion with coach-quarters, which she couldn't quite manage yet.

She became a noted sight in her carefully chosen bonnets and crinolines, whether driving or walking. Once she ventured out on foot to a flower-booth; she greatly missed the garden at Lawley, in which she had liked to sit while poor Clara pruned the roses. Now, Sophy buried her face in an apricot-coloured bunch she'd bought, and was returning to the house with them, when she noticed, in the street, a mounted personage regarding her with great intent. He wore a white hat, and sported dyed whiskers. He closed one eye, but Sophy stared haughtily; this kind of thing was exactly why she'd put in the second advertisement, and was not to be encouraged.

She had her reward; soon, one day, a beautiful lady, no longer very young, called, and enquired about French lessons. Her husband, she said, was a politician. She was announced as Lady Palmerston.

Sophy was naturally on her guard with someone almost as beautiful as she was herself. In youth this woman must have been extremely lovely; her grey eyes were unchanged, though not, by now, quite candid. It would have been uncharitable to say she had a slightly shopworn look, and her hair was undoubtedly assisted by black dye; perhaps her husband used what was left over for his whiskers. Sophy sheathed her cat's claws and instead admired the visitor's dress, which was an unusual and becoming colour of yellow one seldom saw. It clashed a trifle with the velvet of the couch. However the talk was genial, if hardly intimate except in a way.

'I wanted to see for myself if you were as beautiful as my husband stated,' remarked Emily Palmerston, who had to keep a close eye. She added frankly, about the lessons, that although Palmerston himself liked the French and was anxious to come to better terms with them than had for many years been possible in Britain, she would not now permit him to come here. 'If you had been plain or even ugly, I would have sent him, but as it is I will find you other clients,' Emily promised. She accepted a glass of

111

ratafia and they parted amiably after light talk. As soon as she had departed Sophy sent down to the cellar for Ivor, who knew everybody from his days in diplomacy.

'Put that ridiculous harp thing down, pray, and tell me about Lady Palmerston.'

Ivor, who took great consolation from his zither, clutched it to his breast. It had been the nearest thing to a lyre he could find in London. Plucking its strings, he could think of Daphne and send his thoughts winging, on a note, to where she was probably pulling out weeds in the cloister garth. If only—

He came to himself, remembered who kept him fairly handsomely in food and clothing, and gave all the information he could about the Lamb family, from which Lady Palmerston had come although, like most of the others, her father was rumoured to be somebody else.

'Lady Melbourne, who was of course her mother, kicked up her heels a bit,' he related mournfully. 'Prinny said she was the kindest woman he'd ever known, which knowing him means a good deal, and one of her sons called George resembled him exactly. Thing is, George was married, with a great deal of money laid down, to young Devonshire's bastard half-sister Caro, and George Lamb would have nothing to do with her because she was illegitimate. It doesn't sound logical. She's still about, a pleasant little old woman. She knows everybody.'

Sophy asked, as many people not in the formidable and departed swim did, if that had been Lord Byron's Caro Lamb. Everybody had heard of *her*. 'No, that's a common mistake,' said Ivor with some of his former patronage. 'That was Caro William, married to poor Melbourne, who was of course the son of Lord Egremont: he was Prime Minister at the beginning of the present reign. There are a good many Carolines in society, I expect

named for Prinny's bride at the time, before anyone could fore-
see what would happen, and now their daughters.'

Sophy did know what had happened in Prinny's case, and let
Ivor go back to his cellar and the zither. Fortunately, within a day
or two the Duke of Devonshire himself at last called, bringing
with him his plain and pleasant half-sister Mrs George Lamb.
This dear little woman Sophy took to at once, and invited her
back to tea.

'I believe you knew the great Lord Byron,' remarked Sophy
admiringly on that occasion; his works had been in John's library.
Caro George Lamb flushed a little, the colour coming up in her
lined cheeks.

'I would not venture to say I knew him as well as some,' she
replied modestly. 'I acted as chaperone for another lady on one
occasion. She was most anxious to marry him, and had invited
him down to Tunbridge Wells, where she was staying for a little.
We rode about on donkeys with Swiss saddles, I remember, in the
woods, but I kept always a short distance behind, so could not tell
what was being said.'

Sophy reflected that this charming and quiet person would
always by nature keep a little way behind; it was the fate of some.
'Did he propose?' Sophy enquired; she knew Byron's marriage
had been unfortunate.

'No, although Miss Mercer Elphinstone would almost certainly
have accepted. As it was, she married a French officer in the end.
Byron was a small man, and Mercer was tall; also, he did not want
to be thought a fortune-hunter, and she had a great deal of
money then.'

Later, Sophy was to learn from Ivor what had happened to the
money; Mercer Elphinstone's family had cast her off because of
the French marriage, two years after Waterloo. 'She had enough

left from her mother,' Ivor said idly. 'They live in Paris still. She was always fiercely political. At one point she was rumoured to be engaged to Devonshire, but it was denied in the papers.'

Sophy was not quite yet to meet Margaret Mercer de Flahault, although she was soon to encounter that lady's stepson. She was sorry she had missed Lord Byron. Ivor said he was still very well remembered in Greece, which wouldn't have become an independent country again without him. 'They say his ghost haunts the Parthenon.' Ivor had no doubt discovered several such things while in diplomacy.

Clients for French conversation increased all of that year, and Sophy was as a rule too greatly occupied to take note of the fact that the smell of cigarette smoke, which she disliked intensely – pipes and cigars were tolerable, but squashed little ends lying about, and the lingering filth, made her ill – was drifting rather too frequently up from the billiard-room. She complained to the earl about it, who for once proved unreasonable.

'Damn it, Lawley's mine, not yours,' he said. 'I've let you use the rents, but I'll choose my own company.' He bowled off in his chair, and Sophy made friends with him again as soon as possible; it wasn't often that he put himself forward in such ways. She wondered who the company might be; and one day overcame her aversion enough to steal downstairs and find out. Beyond a blue haze of tobacco smoke sat a man not too young by now, with a great dark waxed moustache, hair parted in the middle, and a grey fishlike gaze beneath heavy eyelids. Perceiving Sophy, he rose and bowed; she noticed at once that his legs were too short. Later, she learned that French veterans wept when they saw him from the back and as usual remembered his uncle, the late Emperor Napoleon.

114

The earl introduced Sophy with a rather ill grace. This, he said, was Prince Louis Napoleon, but not to let it be known; as a rule he used a pseudonym. 'Miladi is discreet, I am certain,' remarked the guest with great charm, smiling and revealing dreadful teeth which had nevertheless been carefully filled. The great Napoleon himself, one had heard, had had excellent ones, though he didn't always keep them clean. She noticed that his nephew – there was a further relationship, as Josephine had been this prince's grandmother – spoke with a marked German accent. It was for that reason, he said, that he had originally come here in the hope of acquiring better French; but milord had detained him with talk of billiards.

I don't believe they were talking about only that for as often, Sophy thought, and seizing the bird in hand said she would be delighted to improve Prince Louis' French conversation provided he could manage not to smoke upstairs. The effect on the pale blue drapes would have been disastrous, she decided, even through the closed door.

'I was educated in Augsburg, you understand,' the prince apologized later in the only lesson Sophy was permitted to give him. Shortly, yet another very beautiful woman, not this time from the topmost rung of society, arrived dressed in the height of fashion, rather too much so, and with gold-dust in her hair. She was announced as Miss Howard, and had already met the earl.

She launched at once, as Emily Palmerston (who hadn't come back) had done, into the subject in question. 'I have come to beg you, my lady, not to entertain the prince again. If he becomes infatuated with you, I am lost. I adore him, and have spent a great deal of money in his cause, and mean to spend more. His rightful place is in Paris, where I intend to accompany him when

115

they will let him enter France. At present, all of the name of Bonaparte are banned: his mother the Queen of Holland spent years in exile. The prince himself has spent six years in prison, and escaped with my help by shaving off his moustache. He will try again when the time is ripe. He is the love of my life. I beg you to leave him alone, not to receive him further.'

The blue eyes gazed, tear-filled, at Sophy. It seemed an extraordinary situation. This woman, who had obviously shed her respectability long ago, didn't care so long as she could keep her lover at all costs. Sophy respected her, and promised not to receive the prince again. She would say that she had other clients and the list was full. She discussed the whole thing later with the earl, while Charley wiped the scoreboard clean. He was contented in London, and liked his occupation, as it made him feel important, Ivor being taken up with his zither in the cellar and not often available for anything at all.

The earl was non-committal, but a day or two later Sophy had a new client after all. He had an uncanny resemblance to the prince except that he was bald, with extremely long legs. He wore the Légion d'Honneur, also a hortensia in his buttonhole. The prince, who also had the great star of honour, hadn't worn it openly in order not to be recognised. This long-legged man, on the other hand, seemed determined on recognition. His name was Auguste de Morny, and he called himself Comte, which the earl later told Sophy was spurious; anyone could do it, it wasn't like England where, he might have added but didn't, not everybody could call themselves earl.

The Comte made charming conversation with oddly hissing breaths, and told Sophy his half-brother – he made no bones about it, although he admitted Prince Louis had only been told by their mother's lady-in-waiting as Queen Hortense of Holland

lay in her coffin, and had been deeply shocked – had put himself
forward as deputy in the Paris elections. 'Napoleon's son, when
dying in Vienna, sent him the Austerlitz sword,' the Comte said.
'That is perhaps enough meantime.'

He didn't mean the sword. His conversation proved so expert
that after the third lesson Sophy found herself stark naked on
the pale-blue bed, with M. de Morny kissing her all over so that
his moustache tickled. Unfortunately Charley then came in. He
burst into tears.

'Sophy, Sophy, and I have loved you so!'

Morny rose with the utmost courtesy, indicated the vacant bed,
and gracefully gestured Charley towards it at once. In fact it was
unusual for Charley to come upstairs at all.

'I wouldn't go on with it if I were you,' said the earl later. 'He's
beng financed by a banker's wife with golden hair in the Midi.
Keep out of it till the thing's decided, at any rate.'

His advice was always wise, and Morny was in any case no
longer in London. Later she heard with interest of how Miss
Howard – she had been an actress, and an admirer had left her
a fortune – had financed Louis Napoleon's third, and this time
successful, enterprise after being elected, resigning, then being
elected again with a vastly increased majority. They were safely, or
at least one supposed so, in Paris. In a way Sophy would have
liked to be there; but there seemed fewer rivals on this side of the
Channel, though there still remained curious difficulty in having
herself presented to the Queen. Lady Palmerston, politely asked
in a letter if she would do so, had replied with equal politeness
that politics and society didn't really mix; and Sophy knew of
nobody else elevated enough in the circumstances. The earl
advised her to wait. 'Damned dull at court anyway,' he said,
'nothin' but one christenin' after another, with a vast dinner

given every time. You wouldn't be allowed to shine, believe me.'

She contented herself, therefore, with shining just off Piccadilly, though the conversations in general were growing somewhat tedious.

2

ABOUT then Sophy got herself a new maid with the unusual name of Iris. The girl was pretty, well-mannered and obliging, and had brought good references. One day she came up to say that Mrs George Lamb was outside with the carriage, and would her ladyship care to take a drive with her to Hyde Park to see the new glass exhibition girders going up? 'She says to say you may meet all the world there,' added Iris, and Sophy knew that tactful Caro George was aware of her wish to be presented; she might perhaps meet some great lady inspecting the iron girders who was not encumbered by politics.

She assented with pleasure. Charley was at Scarborough, where he liked to go to see little Clara, of whom he had remained very fond. He had said lately that she was playing with coloured beads on a frame, which helped her to count. Sophy privately thought it would do no harm to Charley to have one himself. Even the billiard scores were becoming too much for him, and one could not offend customers by asking for extra change. Fortunately the other side of the business continued to prosper, although she would still like to fulfil Grandfather Aaron's conditions, and they didn't seem to happen.

She had heard lately from Morny, who was still in Paris and said things were going from strength to strength. His letter had borne the device of a blackbird. He did not specify further, but Sophy learned ftom the newspapers that Louis Napoleon had had his term of office extended to ten years and that his servants' liveries had become increasingly grand. It was no doubt a preparation for something or other. Joining Caro at last in the carriage, she ventured to ask who had been Morny's father; she knew already that his mother had been Queen Hortense. Caro flushed, and looked a trifle prim.

'It is a little difficult to mention the matter, because he is the same man who later married Mercer Elphinstone,' she said 'His name is Charles de Flahault, and he was aide-de-camp to Bonaparte. He – he was illegitimate.' Her own despised and rejected state was not forgotten by her, evidently, and Morny at that rate could have no right to the blackbird. Caro went on talking rapidly, as if glad to be rid of the subject out loud. 'His father was Prince Talleyrand, who was ambassador over here for some considerable time, of course long after,' she said. 'How green the Park is already! The weather has been so very fine.'

It was a small world, Sophy was thinking. Byron, Morny, Mr Laverty and his Syrie – *En Partant par la Syrie* was the song written by Queen Hortense – and the Duke of Devonshire and dear Caro and the other Caro, her sister-in-law, who sounded crazy, could all be strung like beads on the same thread, and counted over. She wondered how Miss Howard was faring in Paris.

Morny, before Charley had interrupted them that time, had said she, Sophy, must come there. 'My stepmother prefers it now to Scotland,' he said. 'She has been extremely kind to me. She and my father have no son, because there is a curse in Mercer's family; they hanged a groom on a holly tree two hundred years ago, and the marriage with my fathr even now, has only produced five daughters.'

Morny himself had a daughter by the banker's golden-haird wife, Fanny Le Hon, the earl had told her. The daughter greatly resembled the late Queen Hortense, and a satire in verse was going round the Paris salons accordingly. It was too coarse to repeat in front of Caro. If only Morny could have given her a son!

Altogether the world was ironical. Gentle Caro George, who never harmed a soul of spoke against anybody, had been badly used by her husband, whereas Caro William, with her mad infatuation for Byron and her loss to all shame in general, had been pampered and indulged by hers. The gods, if they were watching, must be amused.

The twittering of trapped sparrows within the projected great glass dome had not yet made everybody blush by their unmentionable droppings having the habit of falling on display-stands; the glass was not yet fully in place, and the girders were still partly open to the air. 'Sparrow-hawks, ma'am!' had replied the Duke of Wellington when asked by the Queen what to. That story, among others, might well be a part of the genteel chatter to be heard beneath the partly completed roof of what was beginning to be called the Crystal Palace. Prince Albert was said to have had the original idea of displaying all possible products of the manufacturing industries of Great Britain, and the man who had once been the Duke of Devonshire's gardener, Joseph Paxton, had aided him and would be given a knighthood in proper course. Sophy felt that she was at last mingling among the great. Undoubtedly there would be a stand from Grandfather's industrial pottery somewhere. She murmured to Caro that she must look for it; and found it at last, though the great opening day in

May was still some weeks off. Meantime, it was fashionable to be curious. Sophy recognised her friend the Duke of Devonshire, who came forward at once, and raised her hand to his lips. She noticed that he always wore the same gold fob watch, a little old-fashioned now; afterwards she mentioned it to Caro.

'That was a gift from the late Princess Charlotte, whom he loved,' Caro said gently. 'He would not, of course, have been considered as a husband for the heiress-presumptive to the crown, as it was supposed then, but he has never forgotten her, and I don't doubt that that is one of the reasons why he has never been married to anyone else.' She flushed a little, everyone knew the Duke kept a mistress, but it was understandable; and there was his deafness as well.

A tiny plump woman was talking and laughing with the work-men, showing her gums a great deal as she did so. With her was a tall man. 'Come and meet Her Majesty and the Consort,' said Devonshire, who had returned to them, being fond of his half-sister's company when he could obtain it. When Sophy rose from her curtsey, she found herself looking into the tall man's blue eyes.

This was the Queen's husband, the man who guided her in her decisions, though Victoria's own decisive nature did not permit total guidance. Albert, Sophy thought, must have been divinely handsome ten or twelve years ago, when the couple were married. As it was, she herself was drawn to him by a silver and invisible thread, and knew they remembered one another from long, long ago. *We met on Mount Ida, among the asphodels, and will meet there again.*

It did not do to say it. As it was, the small Queen's prominent pale-blue Hanoverian gaze was disapproving.

Polite exchanges were made, and they parted. Sophy was not

to be present on the opening day, when Albert, in the glory of a Field Marshal's uniform, read an address to the Queen following the sound of trumpets, guns, the Hallelujah Chorus, applause, an organ thundering, loud cheers, and the Royal Household walking backwards in a procession which included among others the Archbishop of Canterbury and the Diplomatic Corps. Visitors from home and abroad came flocking; the edifice was packed; the rain, which came on at first, had stopped and the sun came out, and its rays shone through the glass on to, among other things, a small glazed figurine of a woman, placed for safety beneath a smaller glass dome among other items on the stand of Masterson and Bevan Pottery's display.

Sophy saw none of it. Other things had happened, and she was never aware that Her Majesty had meantime ordered that Lady Tenterdowne's name was *not* to be included in royal invitation-lists.

Before leaving, the Duke had caused Sophy to make the acquaintance of yet another man. He was alone, dressed in black, and gave the impression of preferring to remain unseen and unrecognised. He was introduced as Prince Metternich, and Sophy was glad the earl was not present, as he could certainly have been rude. This man had been the architect of Napoleon's downfall, had exiled him to Elba under conditions which almost guaranteed an attempt most desperately to return; then the cage had snapped shut, and after that the Austrian had initiated a repressive régime in Europe which had led, only three years ago, to revolution and shaken thrones. The haughty features assessed her now; Metternich was known as a connoisseur of women, and in the days of his power, during the Congress of Vienna, had had certain flowers arranged daily in his hall to indicate, to any visiting inamorata, what mood he might be in. Times had changed; now Metternich was an exile in his own turn and had fled lately to England. Sophy heard him murmur that he had heard of her French lessons, and was anxious to improve himself, might he call by arrangement?

Sophy, bowing, regretted that her list was full. She saw the cold glint of offence in the Austrian's eyes as she turned away.

'You have made an enemy,' remarked the Duke of Devonshire, whose glance, like that of many deaf persons, missed very little.

It had nevertheless been a memorable occasion. She would try to obtain a ticket for the opening. On the way back she was silent, and Caro said in her tactful, wistful way that the Queen's husband was known to be a model of domestic fidelity.

Le Congrès ne marche pas, il danse, thought Sophy à propos of nothing.

3

SOPHY had decided that London was becoming dull, despite the
visitors crowding in from abroad for the Great Exhibition. Her
clientèle was increasingly raffish. Emily Palmerston had cut her
dead in the Park, not that she could boast of entire respectability herself; everyone knew one of her sons by her first marriage
was really Palmerston's. Albert, that model of domestic fidelity,
would never be allowed to visit; and Morny was in Paris, the half-
brothers recently having decided on mutual and profitable
acquaintance after all. Sophy found herself thinking with affection of Morny, and the blackbird on the back of his envelope, to
which as already surmised he had no conceivable right, being
illegitimate; it was the de Flahault crest his father had been
permitted to use. Perhaps if Louis Napoleon continued to prosper, and Morny to grow rich by means of sugar beet, railways and
Fanny Le Hon, the President would have his half-brother legit-
imised or given some title better than that of Comte. However all
of that was probably in the future.

This was the present and, as stated, dull. Charley was in
Scarborough.

She was in this dispirited mood when Iris the little maid came up, bearing the post on a tray, Among others there was a pink scented envelope, and Sophy opened it first. It had been super-scribed by hand, but stated itself to be from Paris. No doubt it had been enclosed in something else.

Paris, Rue du Cirque, April 18th, 1851.

Madame,

Tremendous things are happening here, as you will have read in the newspapers. I am directed by the Prince to ask you to do us a very great favour, if you will agree. He has left a compromising packet at the Three Mariners Inn at Scarborough, and I under-stand that you visit there occasionally. Would you – he dare not show himself across seas or send an agent, and likewise I must not come – kindly retrieve it, bring it back with you to London, and as soon as can be, I will arrange for its collection there? I hope by then to be able to do so myself; matters are moving extremely fast.

Your friend, Madame, and admirer, as is the Prince,

H. Howard

There seemed a little confusion; it was Charley who went to Scarborough, but one couldn't trust him with anything of this nature. She had better go herself She sent off a note to Olave, as Margaret was no longer in a state to receive correspondence. Might she come and stay for a night or two? It might, she reflected, take as long to disentangle matters and to find the inn Miss Howard had mentioned; that might well be a little way out of the town.

She informed the earl that he would have to manage with Ivor's help till she returned, and herself went down to the cellar to see that personage, who had grown his hair shoulder-length and was as usual performing unhappily on his zither. He was one of those people who, while maintaining potency, fail to grow a beard. He didn't appear for meals these days, and just as well. 'Go to a barber,' she told him sharply, 'and leave that thing downstairs. You are expected to take charge of the scoreboard for a day or two, till I return from Scarborough.'

She was to be glad, later, that she had told Ivor where she was going. Meantime she watched the earl sulkily lay the zither aside, and get ready to make himself presentable. It occurred to her that Ivor and the earl might as well turn the little house into a gambling hell; it would pay equally well, if not better.

She then set out, with Iris, in a hired carriage, and reached the seaside resort late on the following evening.

For some years Margaret Masterson had rented a house near Castlegate, which proved not to be far from the Three Mariners. However Olave said that it was improper for Sophy to show herself at an inn. She enquired what her purpose might be, and Sophy saw no harm in explaining that she had been asked to collect a package for a friend.

'It can be fetched,' said Olave. 'I will send my husband.'

Sophy stared. Olave looked as she always had, only more so. Margaret herself had not appeared, saying she was too old and tired these days to receive visitors. Olave's graveyard slab of a face cracked open in what could perhaps be described as a sated nuptial grin.

'You have not yet been informed,' she said. 'It is not so very long since I married your stepfather.'

Overnight – despite the fact that she was tired from the journey Sophy found that she could not get to sleep, the news having been a shock which sent her mind into ever-widening spirals –

127

she began to imagine what was probably not the case at all; the new connection at third hand with Grandfather Nathan, and the pottery, probably meant nothing. However it had undoubtedly increased Olave's personal interest in what could be extracted from the shares and Aaron's will. No doubt her stepfather, who had not yet appeared, and Olave had merely fallen in love at first sight. It could happen in the most unlikely instances.

He appeared next morning, presumably having been round already to the inn. He carried a well-wrapped package, handed it to Sophy and instructed her to guard it carefully; the contents, he told her, were of great value. She wondered more and more in what way he could possibly be involved with Louis Napoleon and Miss Howard. They were a trifle flamboyant for what her mother's widower had once used to represent, and his appearance had hardly changed except that his hair had fallen out. It gave him a distinctly more sinister appearance than before. He still wore the unforgotten leather belt.

There had been no sign of Charley and little Clara, and on enquiry Sophy was told they were visiting friends. 'As you are here, it would be pleasant if you would accompany us to the pottery,' said Olave, adding that things there were very busy in preparing for the Exhibition, though most articles had already been sent south.

Sophy was not particularly interested in the pottery, but supposed she ought to go. She had noticed, on arrival, a large closed carriage standing outside the door, and it was into that they all four, including Iris, clambered. As Sophy intended to travel straight back to London with her maid, she took the package with her in her lap. It was fairly heavy. 'Be careful of it,' said her stepfather again. Sophy then asked outright how he knew what was in it. He did not reply, but she remembered his silences.

The carriage had meantime left town, and they were bowling westwards. Sophy determinedly opened the package, unwrapping several layers of brown paper. At last she came on something hard; it was a bowl. It was undoubtedly the one supposed to have been buried with Grandfather Nathan. It had a crack across the entire surface, which had been carefully mended, She had by now become not only bewildered, but angry. What had all this to do with Louis Napoleon and Paris? She had, she realised, been tricked. Outside it was raining. The drops of wet began to drip through the roof of the creaking, swaying carriage, whose joints leaked: it was far from new.

'I should like to get out,' said Sophy. The bowl was having a curious effect on her. To dig it up, they must have dug up Grandfather Nathan. It was no doubt valuable, one of the few specimens of his work to show a certain mysterious and unrepeatable glaze.

'The journey will continue,' said her stepfather, emerging from silence. He was placed on the opposite seat, surveying her with an expression she disliked. Olave said nothing. Sophy looked round helplessly for her maid; Iris would aid her. But Iris was sitting with her eyelashes discreetly lowered, manifesting no surprise. She had, after all, delivered the pink scented envelope. One could trust nobody. The rain pattered down, and Sophy grew increasingly less at ease. The day was darkening, and at last – she was getting hungry, there'd been nothing at all since breakfast and she needed to relieve herself – the remembered shapes of the great kilns came in sight. They were going to the pottery, evidently, after all; one had begun to wonder. Sophy clutched the bowl to her, having shed the wrappings on the carriage floor. Whoever had put them together could pick them up.

At first it seemed that the day was unusually dark. Then Sophy

saw that one item had been added to the landscape; an enormous and very ugly gasometer, blocking what light there was.
Evidently Grandfather's notion of reduction glazes had borne
fruit. Sophy hoped the results were worth it, but for the present
was too greatly in discomfort to care.

By the time they had reached their destination Sophy was already
soaked with the drops of water that had trickled down her neck
from the leaking roof, and neither her stepfather nor Olave
showed any inclination to move. The rain was still pouring down
at the moment they drew to a halt, and on emerging the two kept
close on either side of her, Iris walking slightly behind with the
small carpet-bag containing night-things. She hadn't brought a
change of clothing. She had expected to return straight to
London with the package, and now carried the bowl carefully in
front of her, wondering increasingly what it had been all about.
Her instincts were not naturally suspicious, but the whole business seemed odd; and approaching by now were a number of
middle-aged men, some in dark suits of clothing and others in
potters' slops. All of them bore a marked resemblance to the late
Aaron Masterson, as noted at the funeral.

Sophy remembered Elijah, whose hair by now was white, and
Amos, who had aged somewhat less; the rest she had confused
with one another, as was understandable; she'd been as a rule
with Grandfather or else with her governess and dancing-master.
They bowed formally as one, and Elijah, who happened to be the
eldest, held out his hands for the bowl.

'It is of great value to us to have this,' he said in his deep voice.
'It was so irreplaceable there was no question of sending it to
Hyde Park with the figurine. We are grateful.' He spoke on
behalf of the firm. He then invited the party into the main build-

ing, which contained the workshop and Aaron's former office. Sophy was glad to accept; any suspicions she had had were overwhelmed by the urgent need for some kind of water-closet. She whispered to Iris, who nodded and in turn whispered likewise to one of the women in plain caps who had appeared. These were the wives, silent and without separate identity. It was a community here, which kept itself to itself. Commercial secrets, such as glaze receipts, were never permitted to reach the outer world, and the effect was almost that of a gigantic military camp, with kilns taking the place of cannon. One of the wives came forward and said her name was Ann. She showed Sophy upstairs to what had formerly been Grandfather's office. It had contained an iron-frame bed on which at times, when business was brisk, he had slept, and the usual offices had been greatly improved within the last few years. They now consisted of a lavatory in willow-pattern, a jug and ewer of the same, and beyond a large bath, also in willow-pattern, a luxury unheard of in Grandfather's day. 'There is ample hot water,' Ann said. 'The gas heats everything.' Certainly the room was very warm, if not too much so. Sophy made use of the willow-pattern lavatory at once and, on returning, let Iris and Ann remove her soaked clothes and take them away to be dried and ironed. 'You will enjoy a good hot bath,' said Ann, who was evidently in charge of domestic arrangements.

Sophy soaked herself in the bath, passing the time in raising each foot out of the water in turn to admire their shape; not all women had pretty feet like hers. She luxuriated in the hot water for some time, then Ann came in with a tray of cold supper. Sophy's clothes were still not ready, and there was nothing to do but eat supper naked in bed. Iris, meantime, had vanished with her nightgown in the carpet-bag, but no doubt would bring it in due course. Shortly Sophy felt sleepy with the journey and good food. She drifted off to sleep, aware of the giant smouldering kilns beyond the window; their shapes, and the glow from the stoking-holes, were a familiar memory of her childhood.

Next day there was still no sign of Iris, and when another wife than Ann appeared with Sophy's breakfast she asked if she might please have her clothes. They were being ironed, she was told again. Time passed, the tray was taken away, and there seemed nothing to do but have another bath, which she'd do presently, or else look out of the window. She knew what was to be seen outside; workers scurrying by now about the kilns, removing fired ware or stoking more, or else trundling greenware carefully to place it on the inside shelves. She didn't however want to be seen stark naked at that particular window, and turned to the other, the inner one, which had allowed Grandfather in his day to look down unseen on the work going on in the shop; the wedging and throwing of clay, the damping of it in the bins, the shaping later on the kick-wheels; often he'd go down himself if he wasn't satisfied, perceiving something not quite as it ought to be, and would put it right. Now, Sophy perceived something which gave her a profound shock. She'd been told by Olave, when she asked, that Charley and little Clara were visiting friends. In a way, they were; downstairs on the shop floor together, like two children, playing happily with sand and clay, their backs turned, making sand-pies with faces, both of them protected by slops from getting their clothes in a mess. Sophy withdrew in some shock. The whole thing was becoming increasingly mysterious. Why couldn't Olave merely have said the pair were already at the pottery and that she was being driven to join them?

She didn't want to be seen like this, and there was nothing in which to drape herself except the towels or the bedclothes. There hadn't been many of those, because of the heat, Sophy decided to have a cold bath for a change; it passed the time. No one came even yet with her clothes, and she played with herself in the willow-pattern bath for almost an hour, turning and splashing. Then the door opened and Iris came in, still not bringing any clothes. Sophy asked her sharply where they were. 'Pray fetch them,' she said. 'I have waited quite long enough; ironed or not, they will be dry enough to put on for our return.'

A heavy tread sounded outside on the stairs. Iris was blushing prettily, evidently in some confusion herself.

'You won't need clothes,' she said, and Sophy noted rather crossly that no title was used to herself. 'Here is Sergeant-Major Masterson.'

There then entered the finest specimen of non-commissioned military manhood Sophy had ever seen.

He was at least six foot two in socks, which he wore with tabs, and broad in proportion. His shoulders were immensely powerful, his legs strong towers. His barrel of a chest must have sustained many shocks, and she assumed that, like his legs, it was furred with black hair. He had a moustache more glorious than banners, and he wore the undress uniform of a famous Highland regiment which had seen service in the Crimea and Afghanistan, and would shortly do so in Ashanti. Meantime, the sergeant-major was on accumulated leave. His dark and rolling eye assessed Sophy as if she were four corners of a parade-ground, and he passed his tongue across his lips beneath the moustache, striding purposefully forward while the dark kilt swung. As she had already correctly surmised, his parts were enormous.

133

She rose ftom the water to meet him, drops cascading from her fingers and her body. She was Aphrodite encountering, after aeons, Mars.

'We'd better dry you first, luv,' remarked the sergeant-major.

She found that she had lost count of time, or of how many days and nights had passed. Food was brought and they ate and drank together, but only as if it was a necessary interruption to what was the purpose of existing, and yet existence itself seemed to have come to an end in a golden cloud beyond space. Now and again she heard rounds of distant applause, which disturbed her; but his speech was so laconic she could not ask, nor was she aware of his coming and going, only that he was repeatedly here, within her, rousing sensations she had long forgotten, had perhaps never known, would never know again, would be forever different therefore from now on, forever changed from what she had formerly been. She heard herself cry out frequently at the summit of the ecstasy; it was for instants like eternity, yet too brief. After he had left her she would feel her limbs weak as asparagus, unable to support her for a full hour, then presently he would return, and all weakness was forgotten in his strength, his marvellous body, the scar a Russian sabre had left, white and crescent-shaped, among the black hair of his chest. Sophy made her fingers play the piano along it. This experience could prolong itself indefinitely,; there was no other prospect, no other future; the present was all. Ahhh . . . .

She remembered later wishing the iron bed wouldn't creak quite so regularly, Everybody in the workroom must know what was happening. It didn't matter. She was hardly aware of the recurring visits of the wives with trays.

*

The pedigree of the sergeant-major was thuswise. Elijah, the eldest son of old Aaron, had had a son named Hezekiah, after one of the better-behaved kings of Israel. However he proved a disappointment in that his great ham-like hands would not by any means mould or even tolerate clay. In fact he had no inclination whatever to be a potter, and despite every persuasion to the contrary had gone for a soldier and seemed to be much better at that. He had also inherited his grandfather's undoubted propensity to be fertile. Numerous claims had already been made to Hezekiah's commanding officer by women he had got in the family way and whom he refused to marry, saying with accuracy that it was a tie. Olave, being his half-sister, had naturally kept herself informed of his progress, and when it became apparent that Ivor was by now quite useless as far as planning for the future went, she had taken steps to ensure that Hezekiah came home for the full accumulation of leave and did not waste his copious substance elsewhere.

Sophy came to herself one day to find that the sergeant-major had not been with her now for several hours. She was lying in the bath when Olave came in, carrying in one hand a grey wrapper and in the other her husband's leather belt.

Sophy flushed, and put a hand over her breasts. 'Take your arm out of the way,' said Olave, and although she did not raise the belt it was still present, and menacing. Olave took a long look at Sophy's nipples, nodded in satisfaction, and laid the grey wrapper down.

'You may take your time about dressing,' she said. 'Your

135

husband and daughter will, however, visit you within the hour. It
has to be attested by witnesses that Charley has been under the
same roof from the beginning. He will be taken away after you
have all three conversed for a little while.'

Sophy found herself trembling so hard that the bath water ran
into little wavelets, She hadn't dared ask where the sergeant-
major was. No doubt his leave had come to an end and she had
simply been left to find out. She stared down at her nipples,
which were darker than at the beginning, whenever that had
been. She had still lost count of time.

Charley's visit was no comfort. He was pleased to see Sophy as
always, and seemed to find nothing wrong with staying here
forever, making sand-pies with little Clarakins. Sophy had greatly
hoped to send urgently, by his means, in some way to Ivor and
the earl, to say that she was being kept a virtual prisoner at the
pottery: while waiting, she had realised the full and appalling
truth. They would keep her here till the sergeant-major's baby
was born, then finish her off at the birth and claim the child and
the money for themselves as its natural guardians. Nothing less
monstrous could have been their intention in making such elab-
orate preparations to get her to travel to Scarborough, let alone
all that had happened since. If only little Clara hadn't been
present, all ears, with her fuzzy dark hair tortured into two short
pigtails and her profile closely resembling Mr Laverty's, one
could have spoken to Charley with more ease. As it was, he
appeared even more stupid than usual; and Clara, asked if she
wouldn't like to return to her sandpies, said Grandmama had
instructed her to remain. Knowing Olave's habits, it was clearly
evident that her word was law.

They went away, and Sophy cast herself down on the deserted

iron bed and wept. They were using her, she thought, exactly like a Middle White sow, and when she asked for Iris to be sent up with her clothes when the tea-tray came, the particular wife who brought it answered nonchalantly that Iris wasn't here any more, she'd gone off with Sergeant Hezekiah.

That was the final insult, and Sophy cried drearily into her pillow. There was nobody left who would help her to get away from this place, and they'd keep her here till the birth, with plenty of food and hot baths, then say she'd died. Perhaps it would be the best thing, after all.

There followed weeks and months of misery for Sophy. Not only was she pregnant by a man who had betrayed her and gone off with her maid – all that was bad enough – but she was kept close prisoner by Olave, who evidently had full control of matters here by means of her new husband and his Bevan holdings, inherited by way of Sophy's mother. He himself was not seen again, to her relief, but Olave appeared at unexpected intervals, to keep an eye on the progress of Sophy's condition, armed with suitably loose clothing and, inevitably, her husband's belt lest Sophy grow obstreperous. She also left certain improving reading, but no newspapers.

As Sophy thickened she would pass the days in watching the activity of the workroom below the inner window: she seldom read for improvement. Apart from Olave's visits she was left to herself except that Charley and Clarakins now and again looked in, but rescue was hopeless from that quarter. Once she turned and tried the outer window with thoughts of escape, but it was a long way to the ground and she had no money, so where could she go? There seemed nothing to be done but to wait for this birth, then expect to be murdered. She grew increasingly nervous, and began to tear her dresses to shreds at the hem in much the same way as many children start to bite their nails. Sophy was still proud of hers, and of her long hair, which she used frequently to comb for diversion, hearing it crackle.

One day she was engaged in this occupation when she also heard tapping sounds coming from the bath. On investigation they would seem to come from along the pipe, which in turn led out to the gasometer, looming as it did beyond the shapes of the kilns and making the skyline more hideous than ever. Sophy looked out and saw two men with a ladder; both wore green overalls. She asked the wives who brought her food and cleaned the room and made the bed, but they shrugged and knew nothing; no doubt the gas company had sent inspectors. Sophy reflected that it would be easy for anyone at all to put on a green overall and pretend to be an inspector; in fact thefts of valuable grandfather clocks had, one understood, been carried out in this way by men in white coats, pretending to be decorators.

The thought stayed with her, and as time passed it seemed that the tapping assumed a certain pattern; she wished she knew Morse code. There were four taps, short long short long. This was repeated, then a second pattern of tapping emerged; long short long long short long long. When she had got used to that, the first appeared before the second, then the whole thing would be repeated. Sophy wished she was clever.

In the middle of the night, watching the covers bulge over her swollen body, now in its seventh month, the answer came to her. If the short taps were vowels and the others consonants, the taps spelt out Ivor Pallant.

Excitement rose in Sophy; she could hardly wait till dawn broke. The workmen arrived early. As soon as the tapping started, she tapped back, on the pipe leading from the bath.

138

Long short long long short long short long short. *Sophy here.* She then went to the window.

The two were working at the gasometer. The taller of them, who wore a woollen cap pulled down over his hair, signalled. It was not beyond possibility that she made out, even from here, the triangular smile of the Apollo of Veii.

From then on, hope rose in her. She had only to wait.

She was accordingly alert when, one day during working hours, the tap of four sounded at the outer window. The second man in green overalls, who had a narrow face and shrewd eyes, was looking in at the pane. Sophy went over, moving quickly despite her bulk, and forced the frame up.

'See that it is not stiff at midnight,' the man said, adding that his name was Ulick. 'I must not stay long now, lest they suspect. The ladder will be here again then; be ready to leave.'

'They may be listening,' said Sophy, who knew Olave was having her constantly watched. Ulick smiled knowingly.

'They will have other matters to take up their attention,' he said. 'Be prompt; when I knock, open and climb down at once. Have no fear, I am a sailor, and will help you.'

This was comforting, as she had no experience of descending ladders even when unencumbered by heavy pregnancy. She made ready a bundle with her nightgown and comb, greased the window-cords with butter saved from her luncheon tray, and could hardly wait for darkness to fall. What had they planned? That there was some central direction seemed obvious; and no state could be worse than the one she was in. Ulick, whoever he was, did not look like a murderer. She prayed that Olave would not choose that day to visit her; her very excitement might give her away.

Nothing of that kind happened, and Sophy went to bed, still in her clothes, and pulled the sheet high over her in case any of the women came in. At midnight sharp, she heard the scraping of the ladder against the wall: leaped, despite everything, out of bed, and to the window, which she had left ajar, buttered and ready to push upwards. To her relief it yielded. Within seconds she was somehow out, and on to the ladder, with strong hands from below assisting her. At the same instant there was a loud and deadly roar in the distance, and the gasometer went up in flames.

4

'WE were only afraid you would give birth with alarm when the fuse went off,' remarked Ivor, seated opposite in the waiting carriage, which had started at once, leaving behind the screaming women, the running men, and the remains of what should have been reduction firings, their bluish flames quenched with hoses. Thick smoke fouled the air and made it difficult to see, and the horse, which Ulick drove, would have grown restive and out of control in any other hands than his. He was a marvel, Sophy thought; and asked Ivor where he had found the man. Ivor smiled his narrow smile, having meantime divested himself of his green overalls and woollen cap.

'He goes his own way, and is no one's paid servant,' he replied. 'He has been invaluable to the Emperor in various ways.'

'The Emperor? He doesn't look old enough.' She was thinking of the late captive on St. Helena. Ivor raised an eyebrow.

'You are not *au fait* with recent happenings, naturally,' he told her. 'Louis Napoleon is now Napoleon III, Emperor of the French. Morny is his right hand and aided him in the initial *coup*; the entire process has been gradual.'

So that was the central intelligence; and explained why there

141

had been enough money for everything. She asked, with some anxiety, for Charley and little Clara, assuming that they had been left behind in the prearranged blast.

'They are already in France, with the earl,' Ivor replied smoothly. 'He has wasted no time in conveying all your effects to Paris.'

'Even the conversation couch?' She was delighted.

'Even that, though the billiard table had to be left behind. However there are replacements to be had, no doubt. The earl is overjoyed at the way matters have righted themselves, and the Emperor has repaid with interest the sums lent to him during his early struggles for recognition.'

Sophy gave a long sigh of deep contentment. 'So we are on the way to Paris,' she breathed, as the sea came in sight and a small ship, of the packet type, could be seen waiting modestly off-shore.

Ivor's mocking glance surveyed her body. 'Do you want to be seen in Paris in that state?' he asked her. 'No, we are making for the Scheldt, to Flanders. Nobody will trace you there. It is fortunate that the crossing appears smooth so far, although one can never predict.'

It was as well that Ivor had not tried to predict. No sooner had they set out than the weather changed, and the voyage must have been one of the worst since St Ursula and her eleven thousand virgins took the longest time on record from Cornwall to the Rhine, where they were duly massacred. Sophy, wretchedly sick in the cabin, tried to think of the unlikelihood of eleven thousand virgins being found anywhere at all, but was drawn back with immediacy to her own state, the howling winds and pounding grey waves of the Channel. If she had indeed been fashioned of sea-foam, it must have been in different weather and else-where. She felt the life within her move, and wondered if her retching would bring on the labour prematurely. Climbing down the ladder, and the carriage-journey, hadn't helped, and alto-gether she had never felt worse in her life. She thought with affection of Charley and, with tolerance, of Clarakins, who seemed to have replaced her in his affections; it was almost time to send the child to school. Ugh. Sophy closed her eyes, and thought of nothing but existing circumstances. The wind even-tually dropped and they almost glided at last into port; raising her head she could see, out of the cabin porthole, other craft at anchor and, beyond, houses and great civic buildings. They had reached Antwerp.

5

A YOUNG man came on board looking for Ulick, who was evidently his father. 'Mama expects you home by ten,' he stated firmly; he could not have been more than sixteen years old. Sophy, by then wrapped in a cloak borrowed from Ivor and seated, shivering slightly, on deck, was amused by the boy's authority. Ulick winked at her. 'The wife knows I'd be off to the pub if she didn't keep an eye,' he said. 'How do you feel?'

'I am not at all well,' replied Sophy with dignity. She was in fact in some distress and Ulick, who had an all-seeing eye, instructed the youth, whose name appeared to be Telford, to escort her on shore and take her to his house, to stay overnight if needed. Sophy took her bundle of night-gear and thankfully got to land. As she walked up the jetty she felt the pains begin. She hardly noticed the harbour-side house to which she was taken, or the placid-faced woman, evidently English, who took them in and put Sophy straight to bed, seating herself by the bedside restfully working bobbin lace on a pillow with pins and corks. An old dog had greeted them in the doorway.

'It passes the time while my husband is elsewhere,' Ulick's wife stated, about the lace. 'Our son wants to go to sea, but I would rather Telford studied law and stayed at home. Is the pain settling itself? It's a little early, from what you say.' She gave a candid look at Sophy, she seemed very big. It wouldn't be surprising if the birth took place sooner than was evidently expected. Ulick's wife Penelope never asked questions. She put away the pillow lace and went and heated some water. Downstairs the old dog wagged his tail. 'Soon your master will be home,' said the patient wife.

When Ulick arrived home, having visited the inn with Ivor, both men were slightly drunk. The dog gave a last wag of his tail, then fell dead. Ulick knelt down beside the body and wept. 'He was the best friend I had. He was eighteen years old. I was fonder of him than anyone. If I'd been earlier, I'd have been with him. Now, it's too late.'

His wife came downstairs to announce that there was not one baby, but two. Both were boys, and both seemed likely to live. The mother was well.

Sophy disliked the sight of her twins as soon as they were shown to her. The rigours of the voyage, the miserable months before that, and the remembrance of the faithless sergeant-major she now abhorred, all went to contribute to a decision reached almost at once; they would not do. She said nothing, and watched Penelope at her bobbin-lace and even submitted to be given the two children to suckle after a lapse of twenty-four hours, during which time excellent broth was brought and she felt better. In fact she felt well enough to plan. When Ivor came in – no doubt he was assumed to be the father, and she had given up trying to alter the workings of other people's minds – she stated as much.

'I'll have a word with Ulick,' Ivor replied predictably.

*

Ulick's suggestion, and Sophy had known he would have one, was to drive with the children in a covered basket to Ghent and leave them on the doorstep of the Great Béguine, ring the bell and go away fast. 'They will be given an education and taught a trade,' he said, and added that she'd better not tell Penelope, who had a soft heart and would probably offer to adopt the boys herself.

Sophy knew heartfelt relief at this suggestion, and as Penelope was most useful in general with her needle she employed her in altering Olave's selected and suitable clothes till they were slightly less hideous. Penelope added some of her own lace, which should have transformed things, as it was exquisite; but Sophy herself felt flabby, used up inside and out, and resolved to find a dressmaker in Paris. Meantime 'You look like a beacon in a naughty world,' said Ulick thoughtfully. She didn't encourage him, partly because she was grateful to Penelope for her kindness and hospitality. She would be glad to leave Antwerp and get rid of the children, whom Ivor had idly named Castor and Pollux though neither he nor she was certain which was which. Sophy privately thought that from their expressions, they might become civil servants.

They set out in a carriage at last with young Telford at the reins; evidently he made a modest income, till it should be decided what to do with him, by driving for hire between Antwerp, Ghent and Brussels. The babies in the basket – it had belonged to the old dog when he was young – slept peacefully throughout the short journey, and Sophy was able to admire the rising and glorious outline of Ghent in this flat country where trees were rare and, instead, one saw walls, cows, houses, canals, cities all at once. Ivor sat beside her in silence. When they came to the north of the city he pointed out a large park, with zoological gardens. Sophy glimpsed several of the Béguines walking, as a rule in pairs; it was a sight which had not changed since the fifteenth century, and they wore the same stiffly jutting starched white headdresses and blue gowns they always had. 'They do not take perpetual vows,' said Ivor, thinking sadly of Daphne. 'They can return to everyday life after a certain time if the life does not suit them. Meantime, they go about for charitable causes and visit the poor.' He sounded disapproving of such a situation, it combated evil, rather like the late bishop.

As they approached the door of the Great Béguine Ivor, who had got his information from his friend Ulick, said there were over a thousand inmates. He took the basket with the covered twins, who were still alive as they could breathe through the plaited willow, and left the carriage, walking quickly as arranged to the great doorway while the carriages waited. As also arranged, Ivor then walked on out of sight round a corner. Presently they saw a white-capped portress come out, bend and retrieve the basket and take it inside. They drove on at once to the place where Ivor had arranged to wait. He was not there.

'We will wait for half an hour,' Sophy said to Telford; there might be several reasons why Ivor was not immediately available. In the meantime, she promised herself that she would send money anonymously to the Great Béguine. There was no need otherwise to say anything more about the matter. For herself, she looked forward to regaining her figure and some new gowns. Feeding two babies had been demanding, and she'd never do it again.

She put up a hand to hide a yawn, and became aware that young Telford was standing at the carriage window, a note in his hand. 'I was to give you this,' he said shyly.

147

With a feeling of foreboding, Sophy opened the note. It contained a handsome draft on the earl's bank, and a message from Ivor.

I will not be seen in the company of such a provincial fright as you have come to look, it said. *Get yourself a maid and presentable clothes in Brussels. I have sent word to the Hôtel Reine Louise to expect you, and that there has been an accident to your baggage.* He went on to give her the earl's direction in Paris, saying Charley and Clara were there. He himself had other business.

Sophy was outraged. To arrive in an hotel without escort, maid or baggage was to start off at an immense social disadvantage. Fortunately this was not yet Paris. She would have herself driven to the Brussels hotel by young Telford, then would dismiss him with his money. After that, she would see a doctor who would advise her urgently about regaining her former shape.

Brussels was prosperous and well-ruled; they drove through streets less ancient than those of Ghent, and passed carriages more prosperous than their own. Sophy glimpsed a hard-faced old man in polished hessians walking by himself, and to her surprise, was told later by Telford that it was the king. 'He knows everybody,' the boy said, and saluted King Leopold with his driving-whip. The suspicious eyes darted sideways beneath the black wig to acknowledge the salute from a humble carriage-driver. Sophy remembered that this was the man who, once young and handsome, had been the happy bridegroom of Princess Charlotte, whom Devonshire had also loved. The Princess had died in childbirth, and Leopold hadn't been happy since, although he had married again for reasons of state, and had children. He looked a lonely and embittered old man, but evidently governed well. It occurred to her that he was

Prince Albert's uncle. How small the world was, yet not small enough!

She swept into the hotel, overcoming the doubts of the *maître* at her provincial appearance and lack of baggage; what there was, Telford carried in behind her. She said goodbye to him with genuine affection despite his deviousness in concealing the note until Ivor had gone. Then she made herself familiar with her suite of rooms – Ivor had of course booked the best – and sank once more into a comfortably hot bath. After that she rang for the hotel *bonne*, ordered dinner to be sent up and the best doctor in the Belgian capital to be requested to come and see her.

The *bonne* looked doubtful. 'Madame, that is Baron Stockmar, and he is engaged in statecraft. He is a friend of the king.'

'He will do very well,' said Sophy in queenly fashion; the draft was more than enough to pay anybody's bill. She unwrapped the grey wrapper from the bundle, put it on, and told the girl to find somebody to recommend her to a dressmaker. She would, she had decided, make a stay of quite some time.

The Baron turned out to be a stiffly correct and elderly person-age who should not have been sent for, but as Lady Tenterdowne was English he had come. His expression was, however, discouraging. 'I no longer practise medicine,' he explained, while the deep lines etched from nose to mouth did not lighten below his thick grey hair. He wore a starched winged collar which made him stiffer than ever, like the bunches of holly placed under the chins of young girls to prevent them from slouching. He asked Sophy a few questions, said she would recover, and was fortunate to have survived childbirth. He was remembering someone who had not; his master's long-dead bride, the fair-haired Hope of

149

England, encountered long ago in the garden at Claremont, in a Russian bodice with long full lawn sleeves blowing in the light Surrey wind, He, Stockmar, had refused to take part in Princess Charlotte's treatment when pregnant; if anything went wrong, he'd told them, he, a foreigner, would be blamed. If he had prescribed, would she have lived? The diet they had given her was wrong: by the end she'd grown puffy and tired, even before the long, long labour started; then at the end, the loud voice calling 'Stocky! Stocky!' and he'd rushed in in time to find her hands growing cold, with the dead child placed nearby, and had gone for his master, by then in a drugged sleep.

Now, that master was king of the Belgians, and he, Christian Stockmar, Leopold's trusted adviser, to the extent not only to have become the mentor of Prince Albert, the king's nephew and the husband of Victoria, Leopold's niece, but also the tutor to young Albert Edward, the English heir. That boy was difficult, idle and unwilling to obey orders. He would come to no good.

Stockmar made himself look at the other golden-haired woman who sat there, who'd also sent for him. There was nothing wrong with her that exercise, probably walking, wouldn't cure. 'My wife never walked enough,' Leopold still said, years after; he'd never thought of the young second wife, married for reasons of state, as taking the place of the first. Nor had that still earlier episode been a success; before the Belgian throne became a prospect, when Leopold was an inconsolable widower at Claremont, growing camellias to remind him of Charlotte's flesh, white as a flower, he, Stockmar, had taken matters into his own hands with an actress cousin of his own, a German who closely resembled Charlotte. Leopold had liked to sit and look at her, and had made a morganatic marriage with her, but it hadn't been the same; he'd dissolved the marriage with Karoline, as she

150

called herself, when Belgium became a prospect. Charlotte was still unforgotten; the king had brought every possible portrait of her with him from England, and she looked down now everywhere from the palace walls. Was it because this beautiful woman now resembled both Charlotte and Karoline that he, Christian Stockmar, could not bring himself to respond to her? He'd become a dry stick, no doubt; but the dead were dead.

'You speak good English, Baron,' he heard Lady Tenterdowne say. He bowed stiffly. 'I am frequently in England; my duty is about His Royal Highness the Prince of Wales.'

She was silent, and he made himself speak more agreeably.

'I can recommend you to a friend of mine in Zürich, who has a health spa, as they call them now,' he said. 'Nobody can fail to feel better there; the mountain air is bracing. You will forgive me; engagements press, and I am only in Brussels for a matter of days before returning.'

'Give Prince Albert my love,' said Sophy. 'We met at the Great Exhibition.'

The Baron looked shocked out of his undoubtedly sharp wits, and bowed himself out after giving her the Zürich direction.

III
Imperial Glitter

1

SOPHY had revelled in the short river journey, only regretting that the Rhine turned northwards as soon as it did; however she would at that point change to one of Morny's new railway trains, which would speed her straight across France to Paris. She had ventured to send him a telegram to say she was returning, and a charming reply had come to say that he would meet her in person at the station and welcome her home. Altogether Sophy felt uplifted, knowing that the effects of massage, swimming, dieting and walking in the mountains, breathing in the sharp thin air, had restored her former beauty and, what was more important, her figure. By now, she could almost have used once more her early name of Tabitha, the gazelle, except that she didn't want to. A gazelle moved gracefully, but when sitting still on deck would surely not have been as alluring as Sophy now found herself, stared at in admiration even with her veil drawn down. Fortunately she had her Swiss maid, who had been selected for her by the owner of the clinic himself and who was expert at massage. The girl came from the Engadine and had an unusual name; Uni. Her people, she had explained, were a very ancient race who had arrived there long ago by way of Italy, and some of their words still remained in the dialect. Uni was a tall and stately creature, with secret eyes, and, more importantly, her massage was thorough.

They had sat together on deck among the rest, and had seen the heights, the fabled castles, the tiny Rhine herons diving for fish in the passing river, then it was time to disembark, with Uni carrying the light baggage. It still contained only the dresses Sophy had had run up in Brussels; more would certainly have to be ordered in Paris, but meantime she was ready to greet Morny at the end of the journey, which seemed long even at the rate the train had sped, with steam and smuts fleeing constantly past the windows. He had thoughtfully reserved a carriage for them, so they were not troubled with attentions from other passengers, and as the Comte's special *protégées* were brought in a collation of fresh grapes, cheeses of the region and a bottle of chilled wine with two glasses. Sophy permitted her maid a glass, but otherwise they sat in comfortable silence while Sophy gazed out at the vista of flat green France; less flat than Flanders had been, but she didn't want to remember Flanders. Now, a new life would begin, and she would attend the French Emperor's court. She would certainly be the reigning beauty once she was fashionably dressed, but Miss Howard still reigned, in comparable ways, in the Rue du Cirque; one must be careful not to hurt her feelings. The little doctor at the Swiss clinic had conveyed news of the day, and Sophy was as greatly up-to-date in such matters as could be expected after an absence of some weeks.

The train drew in, like Morny himself, steaming and hissing to the station, and Sophy recalled how Morny made exactly such noises in course of his talk; this eccentricity of his was famous, however it had happened. She disembarked when the door was opened by a courteous porter, and with the light luggage seized from Uni they approached the barrier, Sophy waving Morny's hand-written billet in her gloved hand instead of their tickets. They were wafted through as if by magic, accordingly; but on searching for Morny's tall unmistakable long-legged figure and even less mistakable moustaches, all she saw, and her heart sank, was Ivor, carrying a bouquet of hortensias. He approached in his nonchalant way, handed Sophy the flowers, and said M. de Morny regretted not coming in person, but pressure of business detained him. 'I have reserved a fiacre,' Ivor added, while Sophy furiously buried her face in the bouquet. Ivor's discourtesy when they parted at Ghent should have prevented him from showing his face in Paris; and Morny's defection quenched her excitement on arrival.

She did not find Paris an elegant city; the streets through which they drove were narrow, jumbled and dirty. There was scarcely room for two carriages to pass, and on the walls there still fluttered torn posters from the recent elections, many with 'Poléon!' scrawled across. 'There were riots,' remarked Ivor coolly, 'but they were overcome. The braid on the liveries at the Tuileries increased, and suddenly one day the Prince President was Emperor.'

Sophy had meantime opened a little note hidden in the bouquet. *I am informed by this gentleman that you have requested him to meet you alone,* it read. *I am therefore withdrawing, at least for the time.* He remained hers devotedly, M.

Her fury increased. 'I am surprised that you have the impertinence to show your face after your late behaviour, let alone tell me lies on arrival,' she said, her cheeks flaming. Ivor looked at her admiringly.

'Your appearance has improved greatly,' was all he replied. It is now possible for me to be seen with you. When you have visited a couturière things will be even better. More cannot be said at present. I understand from the earl that you have found a school in Switzerland for Clara. That was far-seeing, she is by now of an age when her presence would encumber matters.'

He was evidently informed of everything. She herself had certainly arranged the school for Clara, who ought after all to like it. It would improve her French and develop her bent for mathematics and games, which were beginning to be taught in forward-looking establishments. Ivor was looking pious by now, a sign of danger.

'My reasons for leaving you so abruptly at Ghent was no less than news of the death of my mother,' he said. 'In your state – I had known about it since the explosion, in which she perished – it was not advisable to tell you. As you can now see, my motives were of the purest. Her husband died with her. They were in the Masterson house at the time, with several of the brothers but not all.' He added that Elijah, Nehemiah and Amos survived, with their families.

Sophy could not feel any grief, after all the deaths had been quick, and the world was certainly a better place without Olave. Her eyes narrowed as they drove past the Seine; Ivor by now was the sole heir of the Pallant side of the family as opposed to the bastard Mastersons, with whom Olave herself had briefly been in league over the kidnapping.

'Your surmises are correct,' remarked Ivor softly. He guided her at last out of the flacre towards the door of their lodging, with Uni following a discreet distance. 'From now on, therefore,' Ivor continued in a low voice, 'you will have no lovers except myself. We must fulfil the terms of old Aaron's will, must we not? There is after all the little matter of two children left at the Great

Béguinage, and my friend Ulick can witness the fact that his wife supervised the births.'

Sophy fainted on the doorstep. It was as good a way of announcing her arrival in Paris as any other. 'You will of course continue to be seen at such social occasions as you prefer,' murmured Ivor presently, carrying her in and upstairs on recovery. There was no sign of the earl or Charley, and Clara was out for a walk with her governess, which lady would soon be dispensed with.

2

ANGER was to sustain Sophy through her early acquaintance with the Second Empire. Ivor's behaviour was outrageous, like, she thought, that of a bourgeois husband. He kept her in sight whatever she did, and Morny, despairing of finding the beautiful Sophy available, consoled himself with his long-standing passion, so far unrequited, for the almost as beautiful Madame Beeding de Lezay,* who had a title of her own in England and had been married to a Provençal, now fortunately deceased. So far she was a faithful widow, and the pursuit stimulated Morny to an extent which rendered him, from Sophy's point of view, quite equally unavailable. To be shadowed by a personable red-haired escort might make her envied by other women, but Ivor was assiduous also in bed, and she had taken the immediate precaution of sending Uni out to buy vinegar. In other words, everything was as it had been at the beginning, at Lawley.

She had hoped otherwise to divert herself with occasions at the Tuileries. The Emperor had still not succeeded in finding himself a bride – in fact none of the royal houses of Europe would consider him – and for the time being his hostess was his

* *The Silver Runaways.*

160

cousin, Princess Mathilde Demidoff. The princess also was a disappointed woman, as she could have married Louis Napoleon in the days when his fortunes were uncertain, and had elected instead to play for safety and accept the proposal of a Russian prince, who beat her so hard that she left him. She was now, for the time, effective queen of the Tuileries, but Ivor assured Sophy that she herself must call on Harriet Howard in the rue du Cirque.

This was cruel. Certainly Harriet welcomed her, and so did the ring of important political gentlemen who waited on the Emperor's mistress. However there were no ladies to be seen, and soon it became apparent that invitations to the Tuileries would not be forthcoming any more than invitations to Windsor had been. Sophy wept, Ivor laughed.

'Did you suppose that you were visiting the Pompadour?' he asked her. 'Those days are done. Paris society has its rules.'

'You knew that, yet you told me to go.'

'Naturally; it will ensure that your activities are kept within foreseeable limits.'

He fingered her flesh; they were lying in bed. She still loathed him. He would come to her in the afternoons after her massage from Uni and her bath, She felt his touch soil her; he was interested in one thing only, the fifty per cent share of Grandfather Aaron's money, and she, Sophy, was equally determined that he was not going to get it.

One day, leaving her bath early, she surprised him in bed with Uni, This was too much, and she slapped the maid's face.

'Leave her alone,' said Ivor, adding that he would choose his own diversions and that she, Sophy, bored him and always had. Uni took no umbrage and later said the whole thing was the will of God. She added that she had not told M. Pallant about the bottles of vinegar.

Charley meantime was sunk in melancholy now Clarakins, as he rather revoltingly continued to call her, had been sent off to her Swiss school. At the end of term a report came signed by the headmistress to say that now dear Clara was approaching adulthood, it was necessary for her to take two baths a day. Otherwise she showed prowess at games and had a distinct talent for mathematics. Clearly the remembrance of Mr Laverty was never to be allowed to fade from mind.

3

SOPHY was able to right herself socially by means of a series of unexpected events. The first occurred when she had been out at the little shops in Paris byways, where she liked to ferret and where Ivor, who by now trusted Uni to keep an eye on such occasions, did not accompany them. Among the bric-à-brac in one such shop Sophy glimpsed a small round china box with a fitted lid. On it was the engraving of a little curly-haired child, his hands folded in prayer. *I pray for my father and for France*, it said round the edge. She bought it.

She took it from its wrapping and gazed at it in the carriage as they returned. It was becoming hard to obtain souvenirs of the first Napoleon's son, the King of Rome; all of them had been seized by admirers on his early death. Sophy was interrupted in her gazing by the sound of splintering wood in the street; a wheel had come off a carriage driving in the same direction as their own. A stoutish lady, dressed in white with black figuring, had been thrown violently aside and was protesting loudly in Spanish. Sophy at once got out.

'Madame, I will convey you where you wanted to go, and you may leave your man to repair this damage.' Inside the broken carriage, evidently untroubled, was a young woman, younger than herself; she was beautiful in a strange way, with hair of a glorious bronze which must reach her knees when loose. Remarkable blue eyes, set at an angle which made the outer corners lower than the inner, had been accentuated by a slash of black pencil to accentuate the lower lids. The eyes stared at Sophy with calmness and some amusement. It was evident that the young lady was not disturbed, unlike her mother, who was still fulminating and blaming the coachman. Nevertheless she accepted Sophy's offer with gratitude, and made herself known as Doña Manuela de Montijo y Kilpatrick, and said her daughter was named Eugenia. Later, in the carriage, she confided to Sophy that she had been trying to find a husband for Eugenia through all the courts of Europe. Sophy decided that while Doña Manuela was interesting, she was not very discreet. She dropped the pair at their lodging, and invited them to call on her. Driving off, she wondered why it had been so difficult to find a husband for the beautiful Eugenia. Perhaps there was no money.

4

THE earl lived in moderate luxury in Paris now the Emperor had repaid his debt (Miss Howard had also been repaid) and now and again drove out in an open carriage in fine weather, taking Sophy with him. Charley came likewise on occasion, Ivor never. On the day in question they drove out to Fontainebleau. to watch the imperial hunt. 'They say he has asked the Court ladies to fit themselves out in the rig demanded by the late Emperor,' murmured the earl. This proved very decorative, green with a white curling feather alongside the great hat's upturned brim. They watched the hunt gather, and then a final arrival made nothing at all of the assembled grandeur. Eugenia de Montijo cantered up, wearing a dark jacket fitted to show off her tiny waist and magnificent bosom, tapered pale-grey pantaloons secured by straps under her high-arched little feet, and a flat black Spanish riding-hat tied under her chin beneath the rich, controlled bundle of spiralling bronze hair. She eclipsed every other lady present. 'By Jove,' said the earl. The Emperor's heavy-lidded eyes widened in astonished homage. The beautiful Spaniard's riding proved equal to her appearance; she and her sister had been brought up by their late father to accustom them-selves to unshod mules in Spain.

Gossip, thereafter, brought in by Ivor, was all about the beautiful Spaniard. 'She is Countess de Teba in her own right, and her father lost an eye in the Napoleonic wars,' he said. 'Her mother is a fool, but her sister is Duchess of Alba. They are not nobody. It is said the Emperor tried to make Eugenia his mistress by inviting her for a walk in the gardens, but she brought her mother with her. He has no choice but to marry her, if he desires her so greatly. There is much jealousy at court. Princess Mathilde is furious.'

Sophy thought of Miss Howard, an outcast like herself. That lady was overdoing her rôle a trifle; not long before, she had embarrassed the Emperor by following his carriage publicly in one of her own, dressed in Alsatian costume and lolling on the cushions in the accepted fashion used by ladies of light virtue. Sophy had not visited her again, but shortly a note came round on perfumed paper, this time genuinely from the rue du Cirque.

The Emperor has given me a secret assignment into England, it stated. *Will you accompany me? You are one of the few women of quality who have shown me friendship. I look forward to your reply. H.H.*

Apart from remembering last time, Sophy had no intention of accepting. She had just received an invitation to the great ceremony in Nôtre Dame, wherein Napoleon III, Emperor of the French, would be married to Mademoiselle Eugénie de Montijo, Comtesse de Teba. It was evident why Miss Howard was being sent out of the way; Sophy sent a polite excuse, saying with truth that she had an engagement.

The great church was hung with crimson and gold, the bride was supremely beautiful and, again, not at all nervous. Her shoulders and neck were incomparable, and afterwards she gave the milling crowds outside the first example of the *révérence d'impéra-*

trice, like a great flower nodding and returning gracefully to its stem. Nevertheless the wedding night was not a success; the Empress told her ladies next day that she considered the act of marriage disgusting.

Meantime poor Miss Howard had learned of how she had been tricked, as it chanced before reaching England on whatever trumpery mission had been assigned. One of the wheels of her carriage stuck in deep mud in Normandy, it was necessary for her and her companions to spend the night at an inn, and at breakfast Miss Howard opened a newspaper and read the description of the imperial ceremony, yesterday in Nôtre Dame. Like Sophy herself in similar straits, she fainted. On recovery she insisted on returning to Paris, but it was too late; her house in the rue du Cirque had been rifled, and all her correspondence destroyed. Nevertheless the Emperor did return to her once, having discovered that his bride could make scenes in a harsh voice like the cry of a peacock. Miss Howard, who had never made them, was finally given a handsome mansion out of town, left there with plenty of money, and forgotten. Naturally, society did not call.

Doña Manuela, the Empress's mother, did call several times after Sophy's earlier invitation, and on two of them she borrowed money. Later it transpired that her debts were legion, and the harassed Emperor had to pay them, making it a condition that his embarrassing mother-in-law left Paris. Meantime the lady herself had provided indiscreet information to the effect that the new Empress would never love any man again after a disappointment in youth.

'My daughter was passionately devoted to Count Alcanisez, who cultivated her acquaintance because he himself desired to meet her sister, my daughter Paca, who was already married and with whom he himself was in love,' she said. 'Paca remained faithful to her husband, naturally; but Eugenia' – she still referred to her younger daughter's name in the Spanish version – 'never recovered from the shock to her feelings, By now, she is marble: nothing affects her in such ways.'

Sophy felt sorry for the Emperor, but was delighted when the Empress chose her to be a lady-in-waiting, thus putting an end to the ostracism endured under Princess Mathilde. That lady continued to give rise to spiteful gossip about Eugénie, among the rest concerning an early miscarriage brought on by taking too hot a bath. The child, said rumour, had been born perfectly formed, and gave the lie to the new Empress's vaunted virtue. However few believed the story. Sophy herself, in the turns taken to wait on the young Empress, enjoyed her dry sardonic wit. She did not suffer fools gladly, and Sophy, who knew very well that her own wit was not of the sharpest, said very little, merely carrying out her prescribed duties and listening hard. It appeared that the Emperor was anxious for friendly relations with England, and Sophy did not doubt that that was why she herself had been chosen. It was unlikely that Queen Victoria's disapproval of her was known over here, and even Ivor's acid tongue would not be able to relate it; he knew nothing of the incident at the Great Exhibition in Hyde Park. Eugénie continued to talk of such matters, assuming that Sophy was accustomed to move in English society.

'The Emperor was a special constable in the riots there in '48,' she said. 'He has always been anxious to assist politically and would still be so. It will take a little time, doubtless, to overcome prejudice regarding the name of Bonaparte.' She smiled, revealing perfect teeth, and Sophy reflected that the Emperor's wife was fond of him and loyal to him, although he could not arouse passion in her. Sophy thought it unlikely that Napoleon III had been informed about the Alcanisez matter; but the man was so secretive one never knew.

She herself had to continue to endure Ivor. He was in pettish sulks because Uni the maid announced that the air of Paris did not suit her, and that she preferred to return to her native Switzerland. On parting, she revealed the real reason to Sophy.

'I want my child to be born among my own people, in our valley,' she said. Ivor, already informed, was furious.

'I cannot follow her because of my duty to yourself,' he raged. 'It is extraordinary that she is to bear me a child, while you still show no signs of it. What trick are you playing? I promise I will beat you like the bitch you are if I discover anything of the kind.' His expression was ugly.

Sophy shrugged, and told him that if he left her oftener alone there might be more hope. 'You call it a duty, but it is nothing but greed,' she assured him. At present, she herself was well enough supplied with money, and the earl was generous to Charley. The latter's presence was more than ever necessary for official paternity, but Sophy clung in spirit and in fact to her bottle of vinegar, and began to enjoy the functions at court. There were other things in life than Grandfather Aaron's legacy, and the pottery business had no doubt suffered largely from the damage caused by the blast; shares had dropped sharply, but doubtless would again rise.

She attended an evening reception in the Tuileries gardens, with the trees all hung with coloured lamps. Morny was present, and seeing her unaccompanied came over at once and took her on his arm. They walked about together among the elegantly dressed assembly, and Morny related gossip in his curious hissing voice; it was, she thought once again, as if every now and then he emitted steam from his own extremely profitable railways. They discussed social distinctions, which still pertained here differently from those in England, the latter being less complicated and less subtle.

'The faubourgs, being Legitimist and hoping for the return of Charles X's grandson even yet, will not admit any of us, even my stepmother who is of the old nobility of Scotland,' he said. 'She and my father were friendly with the Orléanists, the Citizen King and his sons, which renders them *non grata*.'

Sophy remembered hearing how Margaret Mercer de Flahault's family had cut her off for marrying a French officer two years after Waterloo. She had glimpsed the lady in question on several occasions; she had dark hair and a masterful profile. It was difficult to believe that she had once loved Byron.

Sophy mentioned having seen the Citizen King's widow, Queen Marie Amélie, wandering about by herself at the Great Exhibition in weeds. 'They used,' said Morny, 'to open both shutters at the Tuileries for her entry, as she was a Bourbon; then would shut one for the entry of King Louis Philippe himself, as he was less well-born. The world is a strange place. Nobody really got on with everybody except my father's father, old Talleyrand; and he betrayed whomsoever he chose as it suited him.'

'Tell me again of your descent,' said Sophy, who knew it already but loved to hear the fantastic story.

'Very well. Old Louis XV was visiting the young girls in the Parc des Cerfs, the abode created for him by the Pompadour as she could not keep up any longer with his demands in a personal way: he was after all a Bourbon. One of the girls gave birth to a daughter, whom the king married to an old nobleman, very chivalrous and well connected, named the Comte de Flahault de

170

la Billarderie. Talleyrand seduced the young Comtesse, who bore him a son who was my father. The old Comte made a generous stepfather and permitted the use of his coat of arms, the black-bird, but unfortunately he was guillotined in the Terror. His widow supported herself firstly by making hats, then by writing novels. Later she married the Portuguese ambassador. My father grew up in time and became aide-de-camp to the great Napoleon. He also seduced – we have a talent for it in my family – the stepdaughter and sister-in-law of the Emperor, who was most unhappy with her husband, Louis Bonaparte. Her name, as you already know, was Hortense, and she was Queen of Holland and my mother.'

The present Emperor's also, Sophy thought; and he does not like the connection remembered, though he has a personal regard for Morny. She found the tall bald man regarding her with a look which inspired her to say 'Let us leave early, and take a fiacre.'

They made love in the fiacre on principle, and in course of it, as they wound through the narrow streets, Morny said the Emperor was going to rebuild Paris. 'It will be the grandest city in Europe, with wide boulevards and many bridges. Come now with me to my little apartment, which I keep secret from most. There is no haste to leave before morning.'

Ivor would be standing waiting, watch in hand, she knew. She was sick of Ivor and his pretended respectability; even the legacy was no longer important. Bald men made excellent lovers.

Morny had to reckon with Madame Le Hon in the same way as she, Sophy, had to reckon with Ivor, not to mention Charley and the earl. The woman Morny really craved, she knew, was the

171

beautiful Madame Beeding de Lezay, and the man she, Sophy, had never forgotten was the undoubted husband of the Queen of England. Nevertheless she took leisure to admire the little secret apartment, while Morny made strong black coffee and they drank it together, while staring at a portrait of a fair-haired woman on the wall. *Sa mère blonde*, those who had known the Empress Josephine had said of her daughter Hortense, Sophy asked Morny if he had ever been allowed to meet his mother.

'Secretly, yes, once at Aix. She hesitated to acknowledge me, because all her loyalty – they say he was the only man she ever really loved – was to her stepfather the Emperor and hence, to her own sons of the marriage, his heirs. Two of the sons died, and the only one left is now Napoleon III. My mother was a brave woman. She saved his life once, by disguising him as her footman when they drove through a hostile town. She was not allowed for many years after the defeat to live in peace. In the end she was permitted to buy a house in Switzerland above the great lake, and at last died there; and her son the Emperor, who had been exiled abroad and hurried back, was just in time to see her before her death.'

And after it, was told for the first time that you existed, Sophy thought. To cheer him she said, remembering Swiss Uni, 'I am looking for an ugly personal maid with bow legs, bad breath and any other drawback you care to mention.'

Morny immediately said he knew exactly such a one, that her name was Sylvie and that he would send her round in the morning.

This was done, and over the next few years Sylvie proved an excellent go-between.

IV

Return to the Sea

1

'A BIRD told me you had encountered Prince Metternich in London,' said the Emperor.

Sophy was astonished at this quiet man's perspicacity. No one except the Duke of Devonshire, as far as she knew, had witnessed that meeting; and Devonshire's visits to Paris since then had been few. In some way, the Emperor had however heard of it; but perhaps not of its unfortunate outcome. As was her habit from childhood, Sophy smiled and kept quiet.

They were in the imperial study, a room she had seldom entered, although the Empress, who was present, had her apartment upstairs. Their wide crinolines, which Eugénie had made fashionable, almost filled the small space. The Emperor heroically refrained from smoking, and had had the ash-trays emptied. Since the birth of the Prince Imperial, and Eugénie's terrible labour, which must prevent her at all costs from ever bearing another child, the relationship between husband and wife had become, of necessity, that of brother and sister, except that the Empress continued to resent the Emperor's other women. However young Eugène Napoleon Louis Charles Joseph showed promise and energy, and his existence was likewise fiercely resented by Princess Mathilde and her brother, who was known as Plon-Plon and who should have become next Emperor of the French had the couple remained childless.

'He is still a power, even after exile,' continued Napoleon III concerning Metternich. 'The young Franz Josef of Austria is by heredity an autocrat, like all his family, and two of them at close quarters will never agree. However I believe that if friendship could be established for us in Vienna, as it has been in England, the Austrians themselves may benefit. Otherwise we will send in our troops to free Italy, which since the Congress of Vienna is anything but free.'

'You have succeeded in Russia also,' put in Eugénie. Sophy lowered her eyelashes and concealed the two ways in which she had been deeply hurt; firstly, the visit, protected by many gunboats, of the imperial couple to the Isle of Wight, where Eugénie had waltzed with Prince Albert, and the Emperor with Victoria, on the grass in a great tent to the strains of an orchestra. A mistress of the Emperor's had been present, and Eugénie had objected to her presence in advance and so a special invitation had had to be sent to the lady, who was the wife of the British Ambassador; but she, Sophy, had been banned by Victoria's own fiat, and for the sake of the budding friendship had made no such fuss as had the Ambassador's wife, and had stayed away, It would have been bliss to waltz with Albert, but it would not have been permitted; and anyway what could they have said to one another? *I would greatly like to show you the Rosenau.* And in reply *I should greatly like to accept; but could we be alone?* It would never happen; and the news from Russia was as bad, for Morny was, suddenly, married. His embassy had been most successful, and that great and limitless country, an enemy to France since the later days of the first Napoleon, was now a friend; Morny's bald head had been glimpsed beneath blazing chandeliers at the Winter Palace in polonaises and waltzes, he had been fêted everywhere, and had proposed marriage over tea to a charming young blonde with dark eyes named Sophie Troubetskoi, said to be an illegitimate daughter of the late Tsar. It made the incredible dotted line from Louis XV complete: Morny himself was said to have exclaimed *Tout cela est naturel!* No doubt; but her own heart ought to be broken. She hadn't, however, like poor Madame Le Hon, sent out black-edged cards and dressed in mourning, at the same time suing Morny for the return of several million francs.

Well, Morny was back in Paris with his little Russian bride, living at the Petit-Bourbon with a large number of Pekingese dogs and monkeys. Sophie was said to have remarked that the French were not civilised. Sophy made herself return to what the Emperor of the French was saying. In his youth, she knew, he and his brother Napoleon-Louis had joined the Carbonari, the fighters for Italian liberation. That was in the tradition of the great Napoleon, who by a series of victories had made Italy aware of herself as a nation suppressed by the Austrians; but afterwards there had been repression again under Metternich following the Congress of Vienna. Now, what was she herself supposed to achieve? The Prince, certainly, had wanted French lessons; but they were unlikely to alter his policy now any more than earlier.

'Your father-in-law the earl is *höchgeboren*, an aristocrat, and may impress Emperor Franz Josef accordingly,' said Napoleon III. He smiled, his grey eyes lighting up attractively; it was a face that could assume sudden, irresistible charm. 'You yourself, I fear, would make little impression on the Austrian Emperor; he has a beautiful young wife, and cannot see past her.'

'His mother-in-law loved the son of Napoleon,' put in

177

Eugénie. Her dry harsh voice presented matters as factual. However it was known that Archduchess Sophic – yet another Sophie! – had never become L'Aiglon's mistress among the etiquette of that stiff court at Schönbrunn, where he head been forced to live. Her husband, an ugly and vulgar archduke, was the father of her children; but the unhappy young man who was the Great Emperor's son had been devoted to her, his short life containin no other women, though many had tried.

It was arranged that Sophy should take the earl, with Ivor and Charley, by way of Switzerland, visit her daughter (Sophy thought she might have a quiet few days at the spa, while the others did their duty by Clarakins) and travel on to Vienna, doing what they might there. On return, they were perhaps to visit certain other persons, perhaps not; it depended on the outcome. Sealed instructions would be given to the earl on departure.

'What they have never forgiven,' that personage said later, 'is not Austerlitz, Wagram. or the great Napoleon's other victories; it's the fact that a jumped-up Corsican, as they thought of him, went to bed with an Austrian Archduchess and gave her a son. The fact that Marie-Louise proved a fool and a bitch is neither here not there. UAiglon had to suffer all his life because of who his parents had been, and all he got from his mother was betrayal, neglect and a tendency to lung-rot. Well, he's dead.'

'I shall like to see the rooms where he lived,' said Sophy. She wondered whom they were to visit on return if the earl's interview with young Emperor Franz Josef failed in its purpose. She herself would meantime do the best she could with Metternich: last time, he had been offended.

2

SOPHY was enjoying herself in Vienna. The short visit to the spa had restored her to full beauty, and it was a relief to be free of the presence of Ivor, who had lately contrived to grow an unpleasant little moustache to be in the fashion. She revelled in her freedom, and in the admiration of the white-coated Austrian officers who were granted a sight of her as she drove round the Rings in an open carriage, in company with the earl. Most of the common people clustered otherwise round the Hofburg, hoping for a sight of the enchanting young dark-haired Bavarian princess Emperor Franz Josef had married for love, but Sophy heard that the new Empress chafed already at the stiffness of court life, in especial the fact that she was expected to wear a new pair of shoes every day.

Meantime, Sophy had remembered why she had come, and had written to Prince Metternich, who happened to be in the capital although, since his return from exile, he lived for the most part in retirement in his castle on the Rhine. She stated prettily that she regretted not having been able to talk with him longer in London some years before, and hoped that, during her own brief visit, their acquaintance might be renewed.

A wafer was delivered shortly at the hotel by a footman, saying

that the Prince had already heard that the charming Lady
Tenterdowne was in Vienna, and would be most happy to
improve on former memories. The wry implication was not lost
on Sophy.

The earl had not been invited, and in any case growled that he
wouldn't cross the feller's doorstep; he had turned Europe into
a police state. Sophy drove, therefore, with the ubiquitous Sylvie,
who had been persuaded to have a few teeth extracted and to
take to peppermint lozenges.

On the way Sophy thought again of Ivor's prolonged absence,
and suspected that he had taken time to visit Uni and their son
in the mysterious Engadine valley. That was understandable, and
Charley had no doubt been able to spend the remaining time
with his beloved Clarakins. However a letter had come to say that
both of them would arrive by water in a few days, seeing the
sights on the passing Danube. She and the earl had, therefore,
taken the opportunity to visit Schönbrunn itself before they
came; Sophy had seen L'Aiglon's rooms, with his collection of
beautiful furniture and the portrait of his beloved Sophie, then
a pleasant and smiling young woman with light-brown ringlets,
and the little Franz Josef in her arms. 'Napoleon's son was a
soldier by nature,' said the earl, wheeled through. 'The only
commission allowed him here was in the Austrian army, his
grandfather's. When it came to calling his first order on parade,
his voice failed; the damned tuberculosis, got by way of his
mother. Before that, and despite Metternich, he would allow only
French to be spoken in his household. He found out the truth
about his father by readin' history. They said in 1830 that if he
had appeared there on a white horse, all France would have
risen; but he was never set free by the Austrians, and instead they
had the Citizen King till they threw *him* out in '48. When

L'Aiglon was dead, every last lock of his golden hair was cut off for souvenirs for idiots of women, and they had to bury him in his hat.'

This is the room where he died, Sophy had thought; and the long procession of bowing and curtseying courtiers had wound past the dying youth's bed, with the Host borne at last, though L'Aiglon had ceased to be a believer. 'Metternich destroyed him,' growled the earl. 'If his bitch of a mother had held out in Paris, with the Emperor on the way to rescue her and his son in 1814, things would have turned out differently. As it was, having got her to Vienna, Metternich arranged her seduction by that one-eyed scoundrel Neipperg. They'd said she could have no more children by the Emperor, but she bore that man two if not three. Neipperg had a wife somewhere. It's all water under the bridge now. Talkin' of water, Metternich used to get rid of those he didn't want to keep by havin' them slung over the side of boats goin' down the Danube. I doubt if he has influence enough these days.'

He regarded her with a steady blue eye beneath fierce white eyebrows, and Sophy wondered exactly how much he knew concerning Ivor. He'd tolerated him in his household with remarkable patience. Now, though she tried to put it out of her mind, the notion of being rid of Ivor Pallant in such a way would be desirable. She was excessively weary of his attentions.

In the days of the Congress and its dancing, there had been flowers placed in Prince Metternich's hall each morning to signify which mood he was in, as she already knew. Now, there were no flowers, so one could not predict. Sophy was shown upstairs, and entered smiling; the clear light from the tall window shone on Metternich's snowy head, enhancing the fact that the Prince had aged gracefully. Sophy, on the other hand, had not aged at all; and he told her so, kissing her hands and guiding her to a spindle-legged gilt chair. The all-seeing eyes looked into hers; and suddenly, forgetting her real errand, Sophy spoke.

'Prince, I am told you can get rid of anyone you choose. There is a man who pesters me and has done so for years. He is coming to Vienna by river.' She told him the date of the voyage. 'He has red hair,' she added. Prince Metternich made a fastidious face.

'It is unforgivable to pester a beautiful woman.' he said. 'If I do as you ask, will so fair a lady perhaps do as I ask, in turn?' He fondled her wrist. Sophy felt herself blushing.

'When you blush, you are like a ripe peach on the wall of my *schloss* at Johannis Berg, near the river,' he said. 'You must join me there.' It was less an invitation than a command. Sophy began to tremble.

'I must go back to Paris,' she said. He laughed.

'Nobody goes there nowadays; it has become vulgarian. This man who pesters you will not trouble you again.'

So he had power still. She allowed herself to yield to him; anything less would be discourteous. He proved an experienced lover, as might have been expected. She downed the recollection of Ivor with ease. Afterwards, she produced, from her reticule, the little lidded box she had found in the byways of Paris, with, engraved on the cover, the kneeling curly-haired child, praying for his father and for France.

'Does not that move you to tears?' she asked, handing it to Metternich. The long fine fingers touched the box, then handed it back. He was frowning.

'I disliked that boy,' he said. 'He was of an independent turn of mind, and would neither take advice nor obey orders.'

You kept him all his life in a cage, she thought; and recalled an episode the Duke of Devonshire had related to her, encountered as he had been now and again in Paris. He had been travelling in Austria, had come to Vienna, and had visited the Gloriette above the palace. A carriage had drawn up in which was a golden-haired boy with his tutor. The Duke had addressed L'Aiglon, who could not be mistaken for anyone else, in French; and the tutor had broken in sharply. *The Duc de Reichstadt knows no French.* Yet the boy who was Napoleon's son had understood every word, but was not permitted to answer. It was as soon as he had come to an age of relative independence, one understood, that his household had been instructed to speak French and nothing else. She did not bring to mind all of that to Metternich, who had snapped the Austrian cage shut when Napoleon's son was three.

She left him, saying she must visit her husband's English grandfather; having also asked if the Prince would not use his influence on behalf of Italy. He had shrugged, and she knew the request was useless.

'Our Emperor would never agree to other than autocracy, which is the only sound form of government,' he said. 'I shall expect you at the *schloss.*'

The earl had been equally unsuccessful; young as the Austrian Emperor was, he said, he had all the features of his Hapsburg ancestry, and would not give way an inch. He had even said that some accident would certainly befall the new Tsar, being a liberal; and that the early sympathies of the French Emperor were well known since his days with the Carbonari and the mysterious death of his elder brother. 'They say Napoleon Louis died of fever in his tent, but there are other versions,' he had added; also that *The Times* in England had withdrawn the dead young prince's obituary from publication. 'It would be impru-

183

dent to ally oneself with dissidents,' this second and very different young man had stated. 'I hope the French armies whack 'em,' grunted the earl to Sophy later. He could not predict Magenta and Solférino, though he recalled the brilliant string of Italian victories of the first Napoleon well enough. He occupied his time with picturing the voyage down the Danube of his grandson and Ivor Pallant. 'They'll have passed Melk; always wanted to see that, and the place where they held Coeur-de-Lion prisoner till Blondin got him out by singin' a song they both knew. There will be a band playin' on board. They say old Strauss has a son who writes better stuff than his father. Wish I was younger.' He waited, fidgeting; but there was no word of Ivor or Charley.

'Perhaps they've missed the boat,' said the earl at last.

Sophy knew they hadn't missed it. She knew what had happened, because the method used was proven. Certain men in dark coats would come to recommend a certain view from the boat's rail, and innocent travellers would go to look; then suddenly there would be no travellers, only the dark-clad men amid the crowd. The river ran broad and deep, and no bodies were recovered from it. It suddenly occurred to her that they must have got rid of Charley as well; he was a witness. She hadn't thought of that, and was sorry. In addition, it meant there was very little hope of acquiring Grandfather Aaron's legacy by now. Sophy spent a further day or two in thought, during which no word came.

Soon she went with Sylvie to visit the Kaisergrüft, to see the greening bronze of the innumerable Hapsburg tombs, among them that of the unhappy boy who had had to be buried in his hat. As they were staring at it, and while Sophy was thinking how

L'Aiglon would greatly have preferred to be buried in France, a deep bell began to toll.

'It is the cathedral,' said Sylvie, who had intelligence. 'It is for a person of importance.'

It was for Metternich, they found, who was dead at last. Among the many who rejoiced the length and breadth of Europe, Sophy did so for other and more private reasons. She hadn't wanted to continue with the affair, or to go to Johannis Berg and pick ripe peaches off the walls, imprisoned forever in a second Austrian cage.

There was still no word of Charley, and by now even the earl accepted the fact that there never would be. He was a realist.

3

SOPHY was haunted by the fact that she hadn't considered Charley might die. She hadn't, come to think of it, considered him at all in any way, from the beginning. It was too late to do anything about it, and pointless to enquire. It was like the people who'd disappeared last century, in Venice in underground prisons or else the canals. She shivered a little, and hoped drowning was as quick as they said.

There was another difficulty; she still wasn't going to have a child. If the inheritance was not to be lost, it must be done within the year, to fulfil the law.

She went to the earl. 'I'm glad about Ivor, but sad about Charley,' she said; she'd always been honest with him. 'As much as I can be fond of anyone, I was fond of him. I suppose I'm a hard person. I have loved certain men as well.' She remembered John Tenterdowne. That, and even Albert, seemed a long time ago.

'I'm not ninety yet,' vouchsafed the earl. 'In Normandy, male peasants get themselves sons for the harvest at ninety-four. I've got Norman blood, so they tell me.' He grinned, showing real, if sparse and yellowed, teeth.

186

'There isn't much time,' said Sophy.

'Well, let's get on with it. After that we'd best leave Vienna. There's nothin' to be done with the Hapsburgs; they're like the Bourbons, learnt nothin' and forget nothin'.'

It was surprising what could be achieved from a bath-chair. Sophy was satisfied with the arrangement. It kept everything in the family, and now they could move on to follow out the sealed instructions from the French Emperor, whatever they were.

That journey took them towards Turin, and as the mountains were left behind the earl said he felt tired. He was found dead in bed next morning, a happy smile on his face. Both he and Sophy knew by then that she had become pregnant. She didn't contemplate taking the body back to England or France for burial, but chose a place at the northernmost tip of Lake Maggiore, so that the earl could rest in Napoleon's Italy. The cemetery was full of slender crosses ftom which hung little bells, tinkling in the wind. He would hear them where he lay. She took the instructions with her, and went on to Turin.

In that ancient city, Sophy at last faced a small thick-set man with moustaches so wide he seemed like a mathematically advancing square. Victor Emmanuel II of Sardinia tried immediately to make love to her, as he did with any personable woman, but Sophy told him she was in the family way and had just lost her husband and buried his grandfather. 'I have word for you from the Emperor of the French,' she said, and gave him Napoleon III's missive. It promised to make war on Austria if the latter's rulers had not seen reason about Italy. It also promised a family alliance.

The small king took Sophy, accordingly, to where a plain pious child was kneeling and saying her rosary in the presence of the most precious of all relics. She had protruding front teeth and a hopeful expression. She was made known to Sophy as the Princess Clotilde.

Later, Sophy wondered if, the war for freedom being won, Clotilde would be happy in Paris. It was a worldly place, and Plon-Plon, the promised bridegroom, was much too old for her. However she seemed happy at the prospect, which was to be kept secret for the moment. Later Sophy saw a photograph of the young girl in her bridal gear, a bonnet tied with a broad new ribbon bow beneath the chin, a happy smile with closed lips and the signature *Clotilde Marie de Savoie Bonaparte*. That was after the victories. Later still, after the wedding night in Paris, Clotilde was to be found unpicking the exquisite handmade lace from her wedding underwear to send to convents. 'Ought to have been a nun,' said Plon-Plon. There were children, however.

By that time, Sophy's own son was born. He was the image of John Tenterdowne, was healthy, and she was happy and also rich. Nothing more could be asked of the world except the company of Albert, by now Prince Consort; and that was forever denied.

Sophy had her son portrayed by a miniaturist at the age of two and a half, naked and clutching a sheaf of arrows. Throughout life he would appear to have been born with a golden spoon in his mouth, and at his coming-of-age was asked to unveil a statue in memorial of old Aaron Masterson, the remnants of whose pottery he had inherited as chief shareholder. The statue was in bronze, showing the old man standing squarely at a potter's wheel, throwing a tall cylinder with an expression of deep fulfil-ment.

By then, Sophy had disappeared.

*

It had happened after the death, four years apart, of two men, Albert and Morny. The Prince Consort died of typhoid in 1861, and Sophy thereafter drank infected water in an effort to kill herself, but nothing happened; it was not yet time. In France, Morny was created Duc by the Emperor in a ceremony at Clermont Ferrand in the mountains, and given a scroll containing, among other privileges, his right to the de Flahault blackbirds. Not too long after that, his wife Sophie complained of a sudden cold wind at their country place of Nades. 'We will never come here again,' she said. Morny died in Paris soon thereafter of pancreatic failure. Sophie his widow was desolate until she found letters to him from a great many women, when she shed her illusions and in the end married Alcanisez, the Spanish count with whom Eugénie herself had been in love in youth. The circle was complete, and Sophy, knowing the time had come, made her son a ward in Chancery and then went to a seaside resort and hired a bathing-machine, of the old-fashioned type on wheels.

The rest of the story, which was never believed, was told by the attendant, a woman, whose mother in her time had ducked George III in sea-water from the same machine and every time he came up, a band played God Save the King. Now, there was no band, as it was out of season; and the beautiful lady who had come was alone on the beach. She entered the machine, declined the use of a bathing-costume, and to the attendant's horror emerged completely naked, with her long golden hair loose and hanging to her knees. 'You never saw the like, and I only wish more of us looked like that,' the good lady admitted. She said nobody would credit what happened next; the beautiful lady – like one of the h'Elgin Marbles, she was, only moving and pink – walked out to the sea, and walked and walked as though she was floating on air; then next time anyone looked, there was nothink there but foam, as though a wave had churned up, then it went away. It was all very well to say she'd been drinking stout again, because she hadn't, it was Gawd's truth as she'd told it, and she never saw the lady more, though she'd left her clothes behind and a pile of money on top, to pay for the 'ire of the machine. It was enough to set up in a little shop selling fancy goods near the pier, which she'd do now because she was getting on, and at least if things vanished then you knew somebody must have pinched 'em, that was if they hadn't been sold.

That summer, on Mount Ida, there was an unprecedented flowering of asphodels: and only a few years after, the Second Empire crashed into ruin at Sedan. An age of civil servants had begun, and the gods were no longer interested; then, again, there was war.